ALSO BY PATRICK F. McMANUS

Kerplunk!
The Blight Way: A Sheriff Bo Tully Mystery
The Bear in the Attic
The Deer on a Bicycle
Kid Camping from Aaaaiii! to Zip
Never Cry "Arp!"
Into the Twilight, Endlessly Grousing
How I Got This Way
The Good Samaritan Strikes Again
Real Ponies Don't Go Oink!
The Night the Bear Ate Goombaw
Whatchagot Stew
Rubber Legs and White Tail-Hairs
The Grasshopper Trap
Never Sniff a Gift Fish
They Shoot Canoes, Don't They?
A Fine and Pleasant Misery

Patrick F. McManus

AVALANCHE

A SHERIFF BO TULLY MYSTERY

SIMON & SCHUSTER PAPERBACKS

NEW YORK LONDON TORONTO SYDNEY

SIMON & SCHUSTER PAPERBACKS
1230 Avenue of the Americas
New York, NY 10020

First Simon & Schuster trade paperback edition March 2008

SIMON & SCHUSTER PAPERBACKS and colophon are
registered trademarks of Simon & Schuster, Inc.

For information about special discounts for bulk purchases,
please contact Simon & Schuster Special Sales at
1-800-456-6798 or business@simonandschuster.com.

Designed by C. Linda Dingler

Manufactured in the United States of America

10 9 8 7 6 5 4

The Library of Congress has cataloged the hardcover edition as
follows:

McManus, Patrick F.
    Avalanche : a Sheriff Bo Tully mystery / Patrick F. McManus.
       p. cm.
       1. Rocky Mountains—Fiction. 2. Outdoor life—Fiction. I. Title.
   PS3563.C38625A98 2007
   813'.54—dc22   2006051273

ISBN-13: 978-1-4165-3265-1
ISBN-10:   1-4165-3265-X
ISBN-13: 978-1-4165-3277-4 (pbk)
ISBN-10:   1-4165-3277-3 (pbk)

AVALANCHE

1

HE STOOD AT THE WINDOW studiously watching the large fluffy snowflakes fill up his mother's backyard. Rose, seating herself at the dining room table behind him, said, "Honey, I wish you'd do something besides stare at the snow. Maybe you need a hobby."

"Staring at snow is my hobby," Blight County Sheriff Bo Tully replied. He was forty-two years old, with thick brown hair and a thick brown mustache, both beginning to show signs of gray. "In January anyway."

Rose set a flat carton on the table. "Come help me eat this pie. It's from Crabbs. They make the best pie. Oh, not their coconut cream or their banana cream. They're all right, but they don't put enough coconut in their coconut cream. Maybe coconut is too expensive. They put something in their banana cream I don't like. It's probably to keep the bananas from turning brown."

Tully sighed. "You plan to eat the whole pie right now?"

"Goodness no, not the whole pie. I offered you a piece, didn't I?"

"I guess," he said. He walked over and sat down across the table from her. Her hair had been freshly done that day and appeared to have a silvery tint he hadn't noticed before. Her bifocals had slid down onto the tip of her elegant nose. She peered sternly out over the top of them, her ash-blue eyes closing to mere slits.

"I prefer you not wear your gun at the table," she said.

Tully sighed again. He took off his shoulder holster and hung it on the chair next to him. His mother frowned. He lowered the holster to the floor.

"That's better."

"So, what kind of pie is it, if not coconut or banana cream?"

"Peach. Of course they use canned peaches this time of year, but sometimes in the summer they have fresh peach. It's heavenly."

She cut a piece of pie, placed it on a saucer, and handed it to him.

"Looks good," he said. "You got any ice cream to go with it?"

"In the freezer. I thought you were on a diet."

"I am. The pie-and-ice-cream diet. You want a scoop?"

She handed him her plate. He went out to the

kitchen and returned with a scoop of vanilla ice cream on each piece of pie.

She said, "Have you seen the monster lately?"

"Yeah, I saw Pap yesterday as a matter of fact. Stopped by his mansion on the hill. I'm sure you know he has a young and beautiful new housekeeper."

"Housekeeper my eye! Yes, I know all about Deedee. She's a nice girl, actually. Why she has anything to do with that old man is a mystery to me."

"He's rich, for one thing," Tully said. "He used to be corrupt and rich but now I think he's only rich. By the way, he seems to be shrinking."

"Good. Maybe he will get small enough a cat will eat him."

"I don't think he will get that small, but he used to be about two inches shorter than I am. Now, I doubt he's much over five ten, if that. You sure he's my father?"

"Pretty sure. Why do you ask?"

"As far as I can tell, we don't have a single thing in common, except for the surname."

"You should be thankful. When he was sheriff, which was practically forever, everyone in the whole county was scared to death of him. They probably still are. Blight County was wide open back then, with gambling and prostitution everywhere you looked, and Pap getting a cut of everything illegal and even some things that were legal. Drinking and dancing and carousing every night all night! It was wonderful! Oh, the fun we had in those days!" For a brief moment, a devil-may-care look flashed across her face.

Tully still had childhood memories of his mother as a flashy young woman. He had heard old men talk about her as the most beautiful girl in all of Blight County.

"Is that where he made all his money, getting a cut off the prostitution and gambling?"

"Not all his money. He and that rascal buddy of his, Pinto Jack, sold their gold mine for a fortune, two fortunes in fact. They had this thin little vein of gold they'd been working and somehow persuaded a greenhorn from Pennsylvania that it would get bigger all the time. And it did! The greenhorn made a ton of money out of that mine. Pap was furious with Pinto, for talking him into selling. Pinto is lucky to still be alive."

"Pap hasn't mellowed much." Absently, Tully picked up the linen napkin beside his plate and wiped pie and ice cream from his mustache.

His mother cut the point off her second piece of pie, placed a dab of ice cream on it, and forked it into her mouth. A dreamy expression came over her face. "Perfect," she said.

Even in her sixties and a little plump, his mother was still beautiful.

"You always were a pie person," he said.

"One of my many vices."

Tully licked his fork clean and pointed it at two watercolors on the wall across from him. "I like what you did with the paintings."

"Yes, well, it cost me a fortune to get them properly mounted and framed. They're very expensive museum mounts. My son painted them, you know, so I had to go first-class. Why he wastes his time being sheriff I have no idea."

"The main reason is I sell only about four or five paintings a year, and I like to eat at least every other day."

"I can remember when you and Ginger built your log cabin out on the eighty. You both figured the place would be self-sustaining, and you could spend your lives being starving artists, you a painter and she a potter."

"I remember."

"What's it been, almost ten years since she died? I remember how she used to follow you around when you went out hunting those little birds."

"Quail," Tully said. He remembered, too. Ginger hated hunting but she went along anyway, just to be with him. She would hold the dead birds and pet them before putting them in the game bag. Sometimes she would get tears in her eyes. He would think to himself, she doesn't have to come. He liked that she did, but she didn't have to, just to be with him in the hills and fields that both of them loved. Well, maybe she did have to come.

His mother was silent now, concentrating on her pie. Tugging on a soggy corner of his mustache, Tully watched her, Katherine Rose McCarthy Tully O'Hare Tully Casey. One of the last three husbands was dead, with Tim Casey maybe still alive but whereabouts unknown. Had his whereabouts been known, he too probably would be dead. He was one of those persons Pap said deserved killing. Pap would have been happy to oblige, if he had ever found him. Maybe he had found him, Tully thought. That would certainly explain Tim's disappearance.

"How come you married the old man twice?"

"I was crazy," she said.

One of the things Tully liked most about his mother was her talent for focusing totally on a single thing in a single instant, in this case the piece of pie she was eating, each bite of peach achieving its own individual identity. For this single moment, her world was peach pie. Tully could eat two Big Macs, one after the other, with no recognition of the fact before, during, or after the operation itself. Perhaps, he thought, that explained the ten pounds he had gained since his last Atkins. He stared down at his pie plate. The pie and ice cream were magically gone. Man, I've got to stop doing this.

Rose looked up from her plate. "So, are you taking the night off, Bo? You should. You look tired."

"Nope, I've got to get over to the office and shake up the troops."

"I know you think you can never replace Ginger, but you should start seeing other women."

"I do see other women."

"I mean women who aren't already married!"

"Yeah, that can be a problem, married women. It's just they can't help themselves. They love me. I don't sleep with them, though. I hope you know that."

"Oh yes, I know that. I did hear about that pretty medical examiner you took on a camping trip up on the West Branch. She isn't married."

"I don't want to talk about it!"

"I thought it was foolish the first time I heard about it. Taking a woman camping in a tent in November!"

"I said I don't want to talk about it!"

The phone rang. Rose got up and answered it. "Oh, yes, dear . . . No, no he isn't. Could I give him a message, if I see him? . . . Really! My goodness!"

"Is that Daisy? Let me speak to her."

Rose shook her head and turned away. "Yes yes, dear, I'll tell him . . . Who was it? . . . And she doesn't know how or where? . . . Just disappeared like that? I'll tell him, dear, if he stops by . . . You're welcome, dear."

Tully was on his feet now, headed for the phone, his hand reaching.

Rose hung up.

Tully's eyes closed and his chin sagged down onto his chest. "What?"

"That was your perky little secretary."

"I know. What else?"

"It seems Mike Wilson has gone missing up at the West Branch Lodge."

Tully slipped back into his shoulder harness, then put on his three-quarter-length black leather coat and his gray Stetson. "Now that you got all the information out of Daisy, Ma, maybe you'd like to go find Wilson."

"I probably could. But not until I finish this pie."

2

TULLY GOT BACK TO THE department well after five. Both the day shift and night shift deputies were either in chairs or sitting on the desks arranged in rows around the briefing room. They were waiting for him. Tully would have felt more secure in his authority if all the deputies had snapped to attention when he entered. Instead, they didn't even interrupt their various conversations.

As usual, his undersheriff, Herb Eliot, was perched on the edge of Daisy's desk, chatting with her. He wouldn't have minded so much if Daisy hadn't been in the middle of a divorce. He doubted Herb stood a chance with her, but it still irritated him to see Herb always hovering in her vicinity.

Tully glanced over to the far corner of the room. As expected, young Byron Proctor, his Crime Scene Investigations unit, was hunched over his computer, hard at

work. Ah, if only the rest of his men were so dedicated.
At least they were all better looking, substantially so.
On a scale of homely, Byron was a ten. He had both
the posture and complexion of a clam, large, crooked
teeth that projected outward beneath a wispy mustache, and stiff brown hair that seem to sit on his head
like a mound of dried hay. He was seriously tattooed
and probably pierced. Tully didn't even want to know
about the piercings. Most people, startled by Byron's
extreme looks, tried to ignore his appearance. Tully, on
the other hand, called him Lurch. He was Lurch's hero.
Lurch was also the most brilliant person Tully had ever
known. Perhaps most startling of all, Lurch even had a
girlfriend, and not just any girlfriend but one of aston-
ishing beauty. The girl, Tully surmised, had to be one of
those rare human beings with a deep appreciation for
brilliance.

"Okay, listen up!" Tully shouted, stomping the
snow off his alligator-skin cowboy boots.

The roar of conversation slowly faded and the deputies turned to face him, few bothering to conceal their
boredom.

"I have to make a phone call and I don't want anyone to leave until I'm done with it. Understand?"

There were a few nods. Tully walked back to his
glass-enclosed cubicle. Daisy followed him. She was
thirty years old with short black hair, brown eyes, and
a compact figure packed enticingly in a short black skirt
and white blouse. Everything about her seemed cloaked
in an aura of pure efficiency, from the perfectly applied
cosmetics to the click-click-click of her high heels on the

tile floor. Tully knew she was madly in love with him, but he tried never to let on. Maybe after the divorce, he thought. Maybe.

"I'm afraid, Daisy, that my mother didn't give me all the details about our missing person."

"She asks questions," Daisy said, defensively. "I don't want to be rude and not answer them. I doubt she'll tell anyone."

Tully stood at the window watching the snow come down. "Ma is gossip central in this town." He looked at the parking area, which contained a section fenced eight feet high with chain link topped with coils of concertina wire. "Daisy, first thing tomorrow, get some of the prisoners to clean the snow out of the Playpen. They can use the exercise." The Playpen was the prisoners' exercise yard. "Anyway, fill me in on Wilson."

Daisy glanced at her notepad. "Blanche Wilson telephoned a little after four from the West Branch Lodge. She said her husband, Michael, has been missing for the last two days. He stormed out of the lodge yesterday morning and nobody has seen him since. None of the cars are missing, so she thought maybe he had gone to the 'Pout House.'"

"The Pout House?"

"She said that's a cabin they have about a mile upriver from the lodge. I guess when one or the other of them gets mad, he or she can go up there to pout. Anyway, she sent one of the lodge's employees up to the Pout House to look for him, and he wasn't there."

"So, where else could he have gone?"

"I guess that's the problem. She couldn't think of

any other place. They have some cabins back up on the mountain, but she didn't think he would have gone to any of them, particularly with this snow. I told her you'd call when you got in."

"I'll do that," Tully said, tugging at the corner of his mustache. "The West Branch Lodge is a pretty classy place. Costs a bundle to stay there."

"Yeah, I don't think Blight City folk hang out there much. Mostly Californians, who come up for a wilderness adventure, except with all the comforts of home. And then some. I hear they have an indoor pool fed from a natural hot spring."

"They do. My wife and I spent a weekend there once. Pretty nice. It was a freebie. Pap had done some favor for Blanche Wilson's father and as part of the payoff, he had Carson throw in a weekend for me and Ginger. Pap was pretty fond of Ginger."

"I guess about everyone was."

Tully focused for a second on Daisy. She seemed uncomfortable with the mention of his wife. "That was a long time ago," he told her.

Daisy nodded. "Here's the number."

She shoved her pad across the desk to Tully. He dialed.

A woman answered the phone. "West Branch Lodge, Lois Getty speaking. May I help you?"

"This is Sheriff Bo Tully, returning Mrs. Wilson's phone call."

"One moment." He heard her whisper, "Sheriff Tully."

Another woman took the phone. The voice was

soft and cultured, unlike the voices in most of Blight
County, which seemed more suited for yelling at dogs.
"This is Mrs. Wilson. Thank you so much for calling,
Sheriff."

"Mrs. Wilson, the message I got is that your husband is missing."

"Yes and I've been worried sick. Sometimes he loses
his temper and storms off and goes skiing or snowshoeing, but it's not like Mike to be gone this long. Sometimes he takes a car and is gone for a couple of weeks
but no cars are missing. If he doesn't take a car that
means he's on the lodge property someplace. I'm sure
something has happened to him. It's very cold up here,
with lots of snow and more all the time. I don't think he
could survive long if he is injured and out in the open."

"How long has he been missing?"

"This is the second day. He got upset yesterday
about seven in the morning. He put on his coat and
hat and left. I figured he'd gone up to the Pout House.
That's a little cabin we have upriver. Occasionally one
or the other of us will go up there and stay if we get
mad at something, or just to get away from the lodge
for a while, particularly if we're upset with each other.
But this morning I sent Grady Brister up to the cabin to
check on him. Grady's kind of our handyman. He said
there was no sign of Mike."

"Anywhere else he could have gone?"

"That's the problem. There's really no place. No
cars are missing. There are other cabins up on the
mountain that we rent to guests during the summer,
people who want more of a wilderness experience than

they get at the lodge. The snow is deep here but we do have twenty miles of groomed cross-country ski trails. Some of the trails go by a couple of cabins, but there's no food or water in them now. I just don't think Mike would go up there, when he could have gone to the Pout House."

"If you don't mind my asking," Tully asked, "did Mr. Wilson leave because you and he had an argument?"

"Yes, that's why he left. It was so stupid."

"About?"

"Oh, the usual thing—money! To be more specific, not enough of it. You know how terrible the economy has been. Well, it has hit us pretty hard. About a fourth of our rooms are empty."

Tully tugged hard on his mustache. "I don't quite know how to put this, Mrs. Wilson, but are you sure the argument was only about money. That there wasn't, say, another person involved?"

Mrs. Wilson paused. "What? Oh, you mean was Mike having an affair?" She gave a brief, surprisingly hard laugh. "No, I don't think so."

"In the case of a missing person, that is sometimes a factor to consider. I'm sorry I had to mention it. Anyway, Mrs. Wilson, I will be up there shortly. It's almost six o'clock now. I may bring a couple of other personnel with me. Would you be able to put us up at the lodge for the night?"

"Certainly. I have a room for each of you. And there will be no charge for lodging or meals either, Sheriff."

"Oh, the county will pick up the tab. Several of the

county commissioners still haven't dropped dead at the sight of my expense account, and I'm trying to finish them off."

She laughed. "We'll at least give the county a good discount. When do you think you might get here?"

"About nine, maybe a little later."

"Nine o'clock. We'll keep dinner for you."

Tully thanked her and hung up.

"Can I go too?" Daisy asked.

Tully was silent for a moment, thinking, perhaps thinking a little longer than he should have.

"No," he said at last.

"Figures," Daisy said, smiling. "You get to have all the fun."

"Not all fun. Call Pap and tell him I'll pick him up in about an hour. Tell him I've got a little mystery I may need his help with."

"What's the real reason?"

"To get him away from his new housekeeper for a while. I think she's killing my old man."

Daisy laughed.

"Then get Dave Perkins on the phone for me. He's probably still at his restaurant."

He walked out into the briefing room. It was virtually silent by now, several of the deputies making a point of looking at their watches.

"Sorry to keep you," Tully said. He ran through a list of assignments for both the night shift and the day shift.

"How come you're giving us our assignments now?" Brian Pugh asked. He was on the day shift, one of his better deputies.

"Because I may be gone a couple of days. Herb will be in charge." He nodded toward his undersheriff. A cheer went up from the deputies.

"And just because Herb is a soft touch, I want you guys to keep your so-called minds on what you're supposed to be doing, preventing crime and catching criminals."

"That'll be the day," a muffled voice said. There was laughter all round.

"True," said Tully. "But I can use a surprise every now and then."

Daisy said, "I've got Dave Perkins on line one."

"Okay, I'm done with you," Tully told the deputies.

"And be safe out there!" somebody said from the back of the room.

"I'm not too worried about that," Tully said. He walked back into his office and picked up the phone. "So you're still at the restaurant, Dave? What are you doing, supervising the killing of your customers with those chicken-fried steaks?"

"Yeah, best and biggest chicken-fried steaks in the world. And folks usually don't die of them until they're off the premises. So what do you want, Bo? I know it can't be good."

"I just thought you might like to spend a day or two up at the West Branch Lodge for free?"

"As I said, what do you want?"

"Nothing much, really. It's just that I've got a missing person up there and may need a tracker. I should point out that the lodge has baths fed by hot springs and even an indoor pool. Be good for your rheumatism."

"Us Indians don't get rheumatism," Dave said. About as much Indian as Tully, he had been nourishing a fraudulent scheme to build a casino next to his café three miles north of the little town of Famine. He referred to his acre or so as the World's Smallest Indian Reservation. As part of his scam, he wore his long gray hair in a thick braid down his back and a necklace of bear claws down his chest. The rest of his costume appeared to have been pieced together out of a wardrobe from a John Wayne western. "Yeah, I could use a couple of days at the West Branch Lodge. By the way, who's missing?"

"Mike Wilson. He and his wife own the West Branch Lodge."

"Shoot, I know Wilson. Kind of an ornery cuss. Heard that new wife of his had tamed him down."

"New?"

"Fairly new. I guess they've been married about five years. You get old like me, Bo, five years is new. Anyway, I'll head up to the lodge right now."

"Great," Tully said. "Pap and I'll meet you up there."

"You bringing Pap? This sounds more like a party."

"That's my plan. So we don't want to find Wilson too soon."

"Hey, I'm way ahead of you on that, Bo."

3

TULLY'S LOG HOUSE SAT IN the middle of a meadow three miles from town. Surrounded by nearly eighty acres of timber, the meadow sloped in the general direction of Blight City. On a clear night, the glow of the city could be seen in the distance. The glow, evidence there were other people in the world, kept him from feeling lonely.

He and Ginger, when they were both in their early twenties, had cut the trees for the house on their own land, the eighty acres Pap had given them as a wedding present. They trimmed, peeled, and cured the logs themselves. Building the house had been an act of love. Neither he nor Ginger ever thought it had involved a single minute of work.

Tully slipped the Ford Explorer into four-wheel drive when he pulled into his driveway. The narrow, gravel road descended steeply down into the middle of the meadow. Ordinarily, he kept the driveway plowed with the ancient Ford pickup truck he had equipped with tire chains and a plow, but the snow in January had been coming so fast he couldn't keep up with it. The Explorer, twisting and bucking, managed to make it down to the house.

Tully went in the back entryway, stomping the snow from his boots. The house was warm. When he was home for any length of time, he heated the house with birch firewood he cut himself, but when he was away, he let the electric wall panels handle the chore. An open loft overlooked the living room. His easel containing a canvas of a half-finished oil painting could be seen from below. He avoided looking up at it. It filled him with guilt and remorse. He hadn't touched the painting in two months. It was harder all the time to think of himself as an artist.

On one wall of the living room hung a large oil painting of Ginger in a white dress and holding a bouquet of wildflowers. There were dozens of drawings and paintings of Ginger scattered about the house, but this one had always been his favorite. Even though neither of them knew it at the time of the painting, something had already started to grow inside her head. Shortly thereafter came the terrible headaches and the desperate operation she hadn't survived. That had been nearly ten years ago. He no longer got tears in his eyes every time he looked at the painting.

Tully still prided himself on being self-sufficient, with two chest freezers packed with salmon, trout, and halibut from his fishing trips, and deer, elk, grouse, quail, pheasants, ducks, and chukars from his hunting trips. He once calculated that the fish and game he accumulated probably cost him only about fifty dollars a pound and well worth every penny. Each summer he invited all the deputies and all his friends out for empty-the-freezer barbecues. He had become famous for his skills as a backyard chef.

He hauled in a duffel bag from a shelf in the attached garage and packed a pair of slacks, clean shirts, a couple of ties, and a blue blazer, for evening wear. In the off chance he might actually have to hunt for Mike Wilson, he pulled a black plastic garbage bag out from under the sink. Holding the bag open, he stuffed in a pair of insulated boots, wool socks, his black wool hunting pants, two wool shirts, a two-piece set of long underwear, a down-insulated jacket, a wool watch cap, and gloves. Then he remembered the heated indoor pool and hot tub and added his swimming trunks.

Not having eaten, he thought for a moment about making himself a sandwich from some leftover meat loaf, home-baked bread, and his own special horseradish, which he grew in his own garden and preserved with his own special recipe. He had once considered employing the horseradish as a toughness test for the department's new recruits but finally decided it was much too cruel. He abandoned the idea of a snack, preferring to reserve his appetite for the supper Mrs. Wilson had promised. After throwing the plastic bag and duffel into the back of the Explorer, he headed over to Pap's. Snow was still falling.

4

IT WAS NEARLY SEVEN WHEN Tully pulled into Pap Tully's driveway, the Explorer's wipers slapping away at the falling snow. He saw Pap's housekeeper, Deedee, looking out the window. The old man had somehow acquired the young woman while they were solving the Last Hope Mine murders the previous fall. She had been working as a waitress at Dave's House of Fry. Then one day she suddenly disappeared. The next time Tully saw her, she was Pap's housekeeper. What she saw in his old man, he had not the slightest idea, other than the fact Pap was filthy rich. Deedee smiled and waved, then turned and shouted to someone, presumably Pap. A few minutes later the old man came out on the porch. He was wearing a black wool watch cap, a tan insulated jacket, and black wool pants. His white hair protruded from around the edge of the cap. He threw a small suitcase into the back of the Explorer, stomped the snow off his boots, and climbed into the passenger seat.

"Nothing like being prompt," he snapped at Tully.

"I had to swing by my house and pick up a few duds. Looks like you'll be warm enough."

"Yep, even got on my insulated underwear and wool socks and pacs for my feet. I figure you got to be prepared. A fella who takes a girl tent camping in November, you can't tell what kind of thing he has in mind for January."

Tully started backing the Explorer out of the driveway. "I don't want to hear any talk about tent camping in November! And fasten that seat belt. This vehicle doesn't go forward until all seat belts are fastened."

Pap started fussing with the seat belt. Never in his life had Tully known an elderly person, such as this seventy-five-year-old one, who could fasten a seat belt.

"Here," he said. He leaned over and snapped the buckle closed. "Fastening seat belts is a very complicated thing and requires years of practice."

Pap expressed his gratitude with a four-letter obscenity. He shook his head. "A lot of foolishness, these seat belts. Every time a person turns around in this country, somebody comes up with some new thing to keep us safe—air bags, helmets, signs and labels all over the place warning us not to do stupid things."

"You're right about that," Tully said. "Reminds you of the time you were hiding out down in Mexico."

"I'm reminded of the time the FBI got to poking around the county quite a bit back in the old days, whining about all the gambling and prostitution. I figured I'd get out of here and go spend a couple of months down in Mexico. Found myself a nice apartment in Guadalajara. It was warm and beautiful down there, with bougainvillea hanging down over the streets and tiled sidewalks. I'll tell you this, Mexicans know how to look out for themselves. In the sidewalk right out in front of my apartment house there was a hole about four feet by four feet wide and eight feet deep. There was no sawhorses set up around it or even signs saying 'Don't fall in the hole.' The three months I was down there, not a single Mexican, man, woman, or child, fell in that hole. You know why?"

Tully steered the Explorer around a drift halfway across the highway. He had heard this story a hundred times. "No, why?"

"Because Mexicans are smart enough not to fall in a hole, that's why. They don't have to be told not to. It's a pretty darn nice way to live."

Pap reached inside his jacket, pulled out his makings, and started rolling himself a cigarette.

"Those things will kill you," Tully said.

Pap straightened up slowly and looked at him. "There you go! Bo, most everything will kill you, one way or another if you wait long enough."

"I reckon that's true. But the smell of those hand-rolls will probably kill me first."

The old man took a drag on his crooked little cigarette and blew the smoke in Tully's face. "Anyhow, you got to tell me about taking Susan on a tent-camping trip in the middle of November." He released one of his irritating cackles.

"Nothing to tell, particularly to an old codger like you. You'd probably drop dead of excitement."

Pap grinned. "Try me."

"Hey, Susan and I are still friends."

"That bad, hunh? Now you got to tell me."

"Give me your word you'll never tell another human soul."

"You got it."

"Yeah, right, as if your word means anything. But I'll tell you anyway."

Much to Tully's surprise, Susan, smart, tall, and willowy Susan, a medical examiner with the most fantastic face he had ever seen, had agreed to go camping with him, even though there was snow on the ground. Tully pitched his wall tent on the bank of the West Branch and installed his sheepherder stove in it. He then inflated a double air mattress on the floor at one side of the tent. He unzipped a sleeping bag and spread it flat out over the mattress. He put two sheets on top of the sleeping bag, and then unzipped another sleeping bag and spread it out over the top of the sheets. Then he drove back to town and brought Susan out to the camp.

Before starting the festivities on the air mattress, Tully's only reason for going camping in November, he heated water for a package of Mountain House Oriental Style Rice and Chicken with Vegetables. Then he poured them two glasses of Ste. Chapelle chardonnay into plastic glasses. "Ste. Chapelle is the best wine made in all of Idaho," he told Susan.

She sipped the wine. "I believe it!"

The sheepherder stove kept the tent toasty warm. Susan had already stripped down to her two-piece set of long underwear. Tully thought she looked particularly good in long underwear. They sat side by side on the edge of the air mattress and ate their dinner from aluminum plates. Afterward they lay back on the mattress and Tully started telling her about the time he had run into a moose calf up on Lightning Creek.

Suddenly she got up, put on her jacket and fuzzy booties, and started out the flaps of the tent in her long underwear. "Sorry," she said. "I've got to go pee."

"She said that?" Pap asked. "I have to go pee?"

"Yeah."

"I don't like to think of women having bodily functions," Pap said.

"Me neither."

Tully went on with his report. "Then I heard Susan walking through the snow alongside the tent. I figured she didn't want to go right out in front of the tent. If I had known she was so persnickety, I would have walked away from the front of the tent myself."

Pap nodded. "Some folks like to be considerate."

"So anyway I'm lying there on my back and the tent is all warm and everything, and I must have dozed off. As it occurred to me later, much later, too late, in fact, the problem with Susan walking round to the rear of the tent, there wasn't any rear to the tent. I had pitched the tent right on the edge of the riverbank."

Pap slapped his knee and cackled. "You can be so dumb, Bo!"

"Tell me about it. Anyway, she stepped over the bank and toppled down through the brush. I guess the brush broke her fall, but then it prevented her from climbing back up. Fortunately, the river goes down a lot in the winter, and the edge of the bed there was mostly river rock, although I guess pretty hard to walk on when covered with snow."

"Mighty hard to walk on, when covered with snow," Pap said, grinning.

Tully blasted the Explorer through another drift across the road.

"So Susan walks up the edge of the river for nearly half an hour, until she finally comes to a place where she can climb out. Snow had got down the inside of her booties, which were now wet and mushy. She stomped her way through the snow back toward the tent. All of a sudden, I heard these footsteps approaching the tent, and I snapped wide awake!"

"Any good woodsman would," Pap said, "if he hears footsteps approaching his tent."

"Yeah," Tully said. The snow was beginning to let up. He shut off the windshield wipers. "I figure it must be Susan, but I didn't realize I had dozed off for half an hour. I think she's been gone only a couple of minutes. Now here's the bad thing. I decide I'll play a little trick on her and let on that I haven't even realized she's been gone. So I lie back, close my eyes, and continue with my story."

"Bad idea," Pap said.

Tully shook his head at the memory. "The flaps of the tent burst open and there I was, rambling on with my story: 'So then here comes this moose calf running right by me, and I think, whoa, the mama can't be far behind. Well . . . ' I opened my eyes. Susan was standing there glaring at me, her hair a wet, tangled mess, with dead leaves and sticks and stuff protruding from it. Her underwear was sopping wet."

Pap wiped tears from his eyes. "I can't believe you're supposed to be my son," he wheezed. "So, what did you say?"

"I said, 'Uh.'"

"Just 'Uh'?"

"Yeah. Then Susan scooped up my pants, dug in a pocket for the keys to the Explorer, spun around, and stomped out of the tent. I was up and standing there in my underwear when the Explorer roared to life. I could hear the tires spitting rocks as it headed back toward the West Branch Road. The next morning, Herb Eliot drove up in front of the tent, helped me pack up, and drove me back to town."

"Ha! And what did Herb say?"

"He didn't say anything. He never so much as smiled. That's why he's still alive. Susan had run the siren and emergency lights all the way back to town. Probably scared all the drunks on the road half to death. No matter, I like Susan a lot. I'm pretty sure someday she'll look back on her little adventure and laugh."

"Sure," Pap said, grinning. "But by then she'll be a little old lady. What good will that do you?"

Shortly after they turned off onto the West Branch Road, a full moon emerged from the clouds and brightened the canyon. Sheer rock walls fell away on their left and rose sharply on their right. Massive icicles hung from the rocks. Far below them Tully caught brief glimpses of the river glistening in the moonlight. After a few miles, he had the distinct feeling the canyon walls were closing in on them. The road had been cut into the sheer sides of the rock walls. Down below them they could see an occasional snow-covered point reaching out into the river.

"Good fishing down there," Tully said.

"For what?"

"Brown trout."

"I never heard of nobody catching brown trout down there."

"You're hearing it now, from one who does."

"Really? How big?"

"Ten pounds. Occasionally, some a lot bigger. You drift a weighted, double-hook fly along the bottom. The double hook keeps the fly from snagging in cracks between rocks."

"How about drifting a gob of worms?"

"Probably work. You have to fish the West Branch in the winter, though, you want the big ones. The big browns in the West Branch seem to bite only in winter. You can catch rainbows anytime but the browns seem to bite only when it gets cold."

"I've never seen any ten-pound browns you caught."

"That's because I release them."

"Release them!"

"Listen, the next time I catch a big brown I'll keep it, fillet it out, and bring the fillets to you and Deedee.

Then you can crank up that fancy barbecue apparatus of yours and cook them, while I sit in a chair and watch. And drink your whiskey and smoke your Cuban cigars."

"Cuban cigars are illegal."

"So?"

"Somehow I get the feeling my cigars and whiskey are pretty safe, if I have to wait for you to catch a ten-pound brown. If you don't mind my asking, what are you packing these days?"

"A Colt Combat Commander, in a shoulder holster. Fits in horizontally, with a Velcro strap. Comes out fast."

"That's a .45 caliber, ain't it? How come you gave up the .38?"

"The bad guys are a lot meaner and tougher these days. And quicker. I keep it locked and loaded. All the deputies are required to wear a vest while on duty. I wouldn't be surprised if some of the guys even sleep in them."

"Hard to believe the bad guys are meaner than in my day. Why—what was that?"

"That rumble?"

"Yeah! Sounded kind of like an explosion. It's getting louder!"

"I can feel the ground shaking!"

Pap scrunched down in his seat so that he could peer upward out his window. "Hit the gas, Bo! It's an avalanche!"

Tully punched the Explorer into four-wheel drive and floorboarded it. Snow hit the roof of the vehicle and dislodged the emergency light bar. Gobs of white sploshed onto the windshield. Tully flipped the wipers back on. They strained at the gobs of snow. Snow, trees, and rocks poured into the road behind them and then spilled over into the river below. The Explorer burst through piles of snow that had slid into the road ahead of them. At last they reached the protective cover of a large stand of trees stretching up toward the top of the canyon. The Explorer slid to a stop.

Tully's hands were still clenched around the steering wheel. Sweat dripped off his chin.

"I thought we was goners," Pap said. He was shaken and pale. "If it had led us a bit more, Bo, it would have got us for sure."

Tully stared at him. "I thought you were smoking a cigarette."

Pap looked around. "I was but I don't see it anywhere. I must have swallowed it."

The light bar was hanging by its wires alongside Tully's door. He pushed it away, got out, and jerked it loose. He laid the bar down alongside the road.

The avalanche was still spilling trees, rocks, and snow down into the river behind them. Pap walked around the Explorer and stood alongside Tully, watching the tail end of the avalanche. He got out his makings and started pouring tobacco into a cigarette paper. His hands shook so badly he spilled most of it on the ground.

"It looks like we may be spending more time up at the lodge than we figured," Tully said.

"We're trapped all right. It'll be a spell before the

highway department gets the road cleared. Like next spring!" He licked the cigarette paper and sealed it with quivering fingers.

Tully walked over to the edge of the road and looked down into the canyon. "Oh no!" he said.

"Don't tell me," Pap said. "I don't want to hear."

"The water seems to be backing up. I think the avalanche has dammed up the river!"

"I hope the lodge ain't close to the river."

"No, it's back up on the side of the mountain. But if I remember right, there's a cabin down close to the river not far from here."

"I don't care if there is a cabin," Pap said. "I've had enough heroics for one day."

"I didn't notice you do any heroics."

"It's what I ain't done that's heroic."

5

THE FULL MOON STILL ILLUMINATED the canyon. Tully cleaned the snow off the windshield of the Explorer and its hood. Then they drove up the road, neither man talking. Tully thought it unusual for Pap to be so quiet. He guessed he was still shaken by the close call. He glanced over at him. Pap seemed deep in thought. Tully turned and looked down at the river, a black streak etched against the snow. Then he saw the cabin. It was down close to the river, with a car parked in front of it. He hit the brakes and slid to a stop.

"What now?" Pap said, irritably.

"There's a cabin with people in it down there! It's got a car parked out front. The river has backed up almost to it! We must have passed the entrance to the access road without seeing it. The water is already over the road."

He grabbed his flashlight, jumped out of the Explorer, and went down the hill in long, stiff-legged jumps, digging in the heels of his boots at each landing. When he reached the access road, the water already swirled over the bottoms of his boots. He hit the cabin door with his shoulder and knocked it open. A boy and girl blinked in the beam of his flashlight, holding up a blanket as a screen in front of them. They both looked terrified.

"Get up!" Tully shouted. "Get up and get out of here! Now! The river is backing up and about to take out the cabin!"

The boy leaped up and ran out the door stark naked.

"Forget the car!" Tully yelled after him. "It's done for! Climb straight up!"

He turned to the girl. She was still seated in bed. The water was coming in the door now and rising on his boots.

"Come on!" he shouted at her. "We've got to get out of here."

She threw back the covers and swung her legs over the edge of the bed. She too was naked. It was then Tully saw that one of her feet was in a cast. She started to cry.

"It's okay," he said. "I'll carry you." He took off his coat and wrapped it around her. The water was now halfway to his knees. He scooped her up in his arms and rushed out through the door, the water splashing up and soaking his pants. Desperate as he was, he still thought of his boots. They're alligator, after all. Water shouldn't hurt alligator. The girl was small and thin but surprisingly heavy. She still whimpered but now also trembled from the cold. He started up the steep slope, his flashlight tumbling away behind him. Climbing blindly, he stumbled and almost went down. The girl reached up and locked both her arms around his neck, taking some of the strain off of him. The bank was almost solid rock and steep, only inches in front of his face. He could feel the sharp edges of rocks tearing at the knees of his pants. "I'm sorry," he gasped to the girl. "I can't carry you in my arms any longer."

"Don't leave me!" she cried.

"I won't leave you but I have to throw you over my shoulder."

"Nooo!" she cried.

She made an oofing sound when her belly hit his shoulder.

The spotlight hit him in the eyes, blinding him. Pap had pulled the Explorer over to the edge of the road, so he could shine the light down the slope.

By the time Tully reached the road he was mostly climbing with his knees. Pap reached down, grabbed the girl around the waist, and stood her up on the edge of the road. Tully tried to tell him about the cast on the girl's foot but couldn't get the words out. She was shaking and crying. Pap reached into the backseat and whipped a blanket off the boy.

"Hey, I'm freezing here!" the kid yelped.

"Shut up!" Pap said. He wrapped the girl in the blanket, picked her up, and set her in the backseat.

Tully turned and looked back, just as the cabin disappeared into the surging river.

After his breathing slowed down, he told Pap, "I thought I was going to drop dead."

Tully got into the Explorer and rested his head on the steering wheel.

"I'm freezing back here!" the boy said, his teeth chattering.

Tully told Pap there were two sleeping bags in the back section of the Explorer. "Open them up and spread them over our two victims, okay?"

Pap got the sleeping bags and spread them out over the couple. Then he settled himself in the front seat and sat there in silence, not even bothering to roll himself a cigarette.

"What's wrong, Pap?" Tully said. "You're not talking." He started the Explorer and began driving.

"I'm just trying to fix an image in my mind."

"You're a dirty old man!" the girl said from the backseat. She had stopped crying.

Tully laughed. "You've just met and already she's got you figured out, Pap."

Tully glanced at his passengers in his rearview mirror. The boy was skinny, with a mop of dark hair that concealed his ears. He was only a few inches taller than the girl. In Tully's opinion, he didn't amount to much. The girl was pretty but, even better, cute, with short, curly, dark red hair, large eyes, and full pouty lips. Neither of them could have been older than eighteen.

"I guess you two probably aren't married," he said.

The boy caught his eye in the mirror and shook his head. The girl snapped, "No way!"

"Good," Tully said. "So what brings you up here, other than the obvious?"

"We came up Friday," the girl said. "We have a little break before the next semester starts."

The boy went on. "We were cross-country skiing at the lodge and Lindsay took a spill and hurt her foot. I took her into the emergency room at Blight City Hospital and they put a cast on it. Then we came back up to stay at the cabin."

"That was your idea," Lindsay snapped. "Taking a girl camping in the middle of winter! I'm a math major. You'd think I'd be smart enough not to get involved with this idiot. I should have gone back to the dorm."

"Idiots are a dime a dozen these days," Tully said. "And what dorm is that?"

"At Washington State."

"You're both students there I take it."

"Yeah," the boy said. "I'm Marcus Tripp and she's Lindsay Blair. We're both freshmen. I'm in pre-law."

Tully glanced at them in the rearview mirror. They both had finally stopped shaking. He could feel something warm leaking down both of his legs. He hoped it was blood.

"Figures," Tully said.

"You really think my car is ruined?"

"It's history, Marcus. I saw it disappear."

"My old man will kill me," Marcus said.

"My old man will kill you!" Lindsay said.

Tully looked at the boy in the mirror. "You'll get

to live a few days longer, Marcus. We're all trapped up here by the avalanche. It blocked the road behind us, as well as the river."

"Oh, that is just great!" Lindsay said. "So I'm stuck up here!"

"Afraid so," Tully said. "I suspect the avalanche also took out the power poles and probably the telephones lines, too. We'll find out when we get to the lodge."

6

THE LODGE SUDDENLY APPEARED, DARK and massive above them. It was four stories high, with sections of logs holding up the roof of a vast covered veranda that swept around the main building. Several windows had dim yellowish lights illuminating them. There were similar lights in the portion of the building Tully knew to be the dining room.

The parking lot was crammed with vehicles, most of them SUVs. As they pulled into the lot, they drove over a packed section of the new snow. The headlights picked up a red spray. He stopped and backed up. Both he and Pap leaned forward to study the trampled snow.

Tully said, "Looks like blood to me."

Pap said, "From my vast experience with blood, I'd say this comes from a fistfight."

"I think you may be right." Tully backed into an opening between a Yukon and a Lexus sport utility vehicle. "I'll go in and see if I can round up some clothes for these two. And a pair of crutches."

Lindsay said, "I still have a room here. All my stuff is still in my room, number 222. They can get me some clothes from there."

"I have a room too," Marcus said. "Room 318."

"You each have a room?" Tully asked. "So what were you doing in the cabin?"

"I thought it would be romantic," Marcus said.

Tully shook his head. "I hope you realize now, Marcus, that romance is not what it's cracked up to be."

"Yeah."

"Okay then," Tully said. "So all we need is crutches for you, Lindsay, and some bathrobes or something so you can get to your rooms."

"You actually think they'll have crutches?" Lindsay said.

"They ski here, don't they? Of course they'll have crutches."

He got out and walked up to the lodge. Even in the dark, it was impressive.

Built in the Twenties, the outer walls had been constructed of stones and logs. He vaguely recalled that a couple of movies had been filmed there. One of the massive doors swung open at scarcely more than the touch of his hand on the handle. A forest of candles illuminated the foyer but nobody was at what he took to be a registration desk. He walked toward the sound of voices and into a lounge area. He stopped a young woman. She was wearing a green jacket with a West Branch Lodge emblem on it. "Ah, you work here," he said.

"If anyone is watching," she said. "I'm Wendy Curtis. What can I do for you?"

Tully explained about the crutches and bathrobes or other covering for Lindsay and Marcus to get to their rooms. He gave her the room numbers.

"You look as if you could use some new clothes yourself, Sheriff."

"Not as badly as I need a stiff drink, Wendy."

"The bar is just around the corner. I'll take care of the robes and crutches."

Tully thanked her and walked into the lounge. A bar ran along the wall to his left. At the far end, a tall, stocky bartender leaned over it in intense conversation with a young woman. Whatever he was selling, the woman wasn't buying it. She actually stomped her foot at one point. She wore a leather jacket and jeans and even in the dim light Tully rated her somewhere between very cute and gorgeous.

Tully called down to the bartender. "Excuse me, but could I get a drink here?"

The bartender glared at him. "Can't you see I'm busy!" he snapped. He went back to arguing with the woman.

Tully grabbed the bartender by the hair and smashed his face up and down on the bar. But only in his mind. The man had a neck thick as a rhino's.

Nothing is more embarrassing than grabbing a hand-ful of hair and then not being able to move a man's head. This had never happened to Tully and he didn't intend for it to.

At last the woman pushed back from the bar, still shaking her head, and stormed off. He thought he detected cheeks glistening with tears when she went by him. Another good reason to whomp the bartender's face up and down on the bar. Perhaps they were hav-ing a lovers' quarrel. The bartender couldn't have been out of his twenties. A lock of dark hair curled down onto his forehead. Youth. Muscle. Looks. It was hard to imagine a more disgusting combination. The man came down the bar toward him, his demeanor suggest-ing menace.

"So?" he said.

Tully undid the badge from his belt and laid it on the bar. "What will that buy me?"

"Oh-oh," the bartender said. "You must be Sheriff Tully. You have to admit you're kind of a mess."

"Mess or not, I'm young Sheriff Tully. If I were old Sheriff Tully, you'd be dead by now. Or wishing you were."

"I'm sorry. I mistook you for one of the locals."

"The locals?"

"Yeah, they're kind of a rough lot—no offense. The mountains back here are full of them. We had one in a few nights ago, got drunk, did a striptease right in front of everybody. I chased him all over the ballroom, him giggling like a fool and jumping from table to table. I dragged him stark naked out the door and threw him down the front steps. He probably froze to death. I hope he did, anyway. Is that a crime, Sheriff?"

"Hey, you're talking about my life."

The bartender held a thick hand out over the bar. "DeWayne Scragg," he said.

Tully shook the hand. "Bo Tully," he said. "You by any chance related to Batim Scragg?" Batim owned a run-down ranch up north of the little town of Famine. At the moment, Tully had his two sons in jail on a drug charge connected with the Last Hope murders.

"He's some relation but I won't admit what," DeWayne said.

"Oh, Batim isn't such a bad sort," Tully said. "I put him in prison once and my old man put him in once. You get to know him, he's a pretty decent fellow."

"You like Scotch, Sheriff?"

"Single malt, if you have it."

DeWayne took a glass off a shelf and filled it with Glenfiddich. He set the glass in front of Tully. "On the house, Sheriff."

"I appreciate it, DeWayne. But run a tab for me and my men. They'll let you know who they are."

"One of them already has. An Indian fellow. Said you'd be running a tab."

An Indian fellow. Tully took a sip of Scotch and smiled. "You mixed it just right, DeWayne. Tell me, you got any idea where Mike Wilson could have gone?"

The bartender frowned. "Mike runs off like this fairly often. Stays gone for a week or so and then comes back."

"So why is Mrs. Wilson so upset this time. He's been gone only a couple of days."

"Because he didn't take a car. She figured he had skied up to the Pout House. That's a—"

"I know," Tully said. "I take it Mike Wilson isn't so good to the help?"

"He treats me all right, but he has a mean streak. He gives the women a pretty rough time. Bawls out the waitresses in front of everybody. If you don't do everything exactly as he wants it done, he goes bananas. Except you never know how he wants it done until you've done it. What's the word for that? Compulsive something."

"Obsessive. Compulsive obsessive. It's one of the most irritating of mental disorders. Not to the victim but to everybody else. He ever hit anybody?"

The bartender was silent for a moment, obviously thinking over his response. "Not the help, not that I know of anyway."

"Not the help. How about somebody who isn't help?"

DeWayne looked around, then leaned across the bar toward Tully. "Mrs. Wilson didn't come out of her apartment for a couple of days. I asked Wendy, one of the housekeeping persons, to check on her. She told me Mrs. Wilson had been beaten up. Had two black eyes and a puffy lip."

"You think Mike Wilson did it?"

"I had a little talk with Mike about it. There's been no evidence Mrs. Wilson has ever been hit again."

"Odd that Mike didn't fire you after your little talk," Tully said.

"He probably would have if he could. I think Mrs. Wilson holds all the cards. Also, I'm sort of connected around these parts."

"I take it you mean you're part of the Scragg family."

"Did I say that?"

Tully took a sip of his Scotch. "If Mike doesn't hit the help, does he ever hit on them?"

"Yeah, there's some of that. Maybe some more serious stuff, too, but I don't know. Some of the girls are terrified of him. They would probably quit but jobs are scarce around here."

Tully took another sip of his Scotch. "You think something has happened to Wilson?"

"We've checked all the cabins, and there's no sign he's been in any of them. Up here this time of year, a man can't be outside for two days and live. I figure he's dead. Fell and broke a leg and froze, something like that. Has to be, unless he's holed up in a snow cave somewhere."

"Well, I'd better be moseying along. Nice talking to you, DeWayne. By the way, when I walked up I noticed you seemed to be having some lady trouble. The young woman was pretty upset. What was that all about, if you don't mind my asking?"

The bartender seemed startled by the question, but then said, "No, I don't mind. Alice is my girlfriend. Was my girlfriend. It's over now. I told her I've got some plans and it just wasn't possible for her to be part of them. If you've ever been romantically involved, Sheriff, you'd understand."

"Romance is much too complicated for me, DeWayne. I prefer to leave that sort of misery to you young fellows."

He thanked the bartender for the information and wandered into the dining room. Lit only by candles, the room was dim and smoky. It was occupied with perhaps thirty people at white-clothed tables. The diners kept their talk to a low murmur, as if they were at the scene of an accident.

A soft voice behind him said, "You must be Sheriff Tully. I'm Mrs. Wilson."

He turned. She was a small, elegant woman in a black dress, pearl necklace, matching pearl earrings, and a pair of gold-rimmed reading glasses dangling from a thin gold chain. She wore her silvery hair in a chic cut. He guessed she might be fifty.

"I am he," Tully said.

"You are something of a mess, I must say."

"I've had a trying day."

"We also," she said. "As you can see, we lost our electricity a short while ago. I would suspect Mike, but I can hardly believe he is that upset with me. He does have a rather fierce temper, though."

"I can assure you Mike is innocent of the electrical problem. An avalanche very nearly got us on our way in, and I'm quite sure it wiped out your power lines."

"Good heavens!" she said. "That explains why our phones are dead, too."

"I'm afraid so. One of your employees, a nice lady

by the name of Wendy Curtis, has arranged to get a couple of my young passengers back to their rooms, as well as find the girl a pair of crutches."

"A new set of clothes might be in order for you, Sheriff."

"I guess," he said. "Actually, I have some extra duds in the car. They're in a large duffel bag in the back of my vehicle, a red, battered Ford Explorer with a sheriff's insignia on the side. Maybe you could have someone haul the bag up to a room."

"I'll get that taken care of right away. But first, Sheriff, maybe you would like to step into my office for a few moments. You seem to be dripping blood on the floor."

Tully glanced down. There were several bright red spots on the floorboards. He followed Mrs. Wilson into her office. She pulled a chair out and gave him a gentle push into it. "Now, if you will please drop your pants," she said.

Tully was too exhausted to be shocked. He undid his belt and slid his pants down. His knees were a bloody mess. He could hardly stand to look at them. Mrs. Wilson ran some warm water in a pan and came back and knelt in from of him. She carefully dabbed away the blood and then took a dropper from a small, dark bottle of something and dribbled the liquid over the raw places. Tully let on as if he felt nothing, although his first impulse was to rise screeching from the chair.

"I hope this doesn't hurt too much," Mrs. Wilson said. "It should take care of any infection, though."

"Mmm," Tully said, shaking his head. He could feel his eyes tearing up.

She dabbed his knees with gauze and then taped squares of gauze over each. "Knees are so hard to bandage but there, that should hold them for a while."

"Thanks," Tully croaked. "That's very kind of you."

"You're welcome. Usually I wait at least an hour after I meet a man before I ask him to drop his pants. Now you have to tell me how you ever managed to do that to your knees."

"How about later?" he said. "Right now I'd like to change into my other clothes. And maybe have another large drink with some dinner."

"It'll be waiting for you."

7

HIS ROOM WAS NICER THAN he had expected. Half a dozen candles provided a soft, glowing light. The furnishings were clearly old but well cared for. The double bed appeared to be made out of peeled, varnished poles. A matching nightstand was on each side of the bed. Large braided rugs covered most of the floor. Four straight-backed chairs were arranged around a small wooden table. A large wood-and-leather rocking chair completed the furnishings. In the bath, someone had placed a bucket of water next to the toilet, apparently for flushing, if the electricity failed to come on anytime soon. He was particularly pleased at the sight of a massive, claw-foot tub. The sink was equally old and impressive, with a large mirror above it. Tully looked in the mirror. It was a mistake. He shuddered at the sight of himself. He grabbed the bucket of water, splashed the sink full, then washed his face and hands, combed his hair and mustache, and headed downstairs for dinner.

As he entered the lounge, the lights came back on with blinding brightness. Tully actually preferred the candles and was confused as to how the electricity could be restored so quickly after the avalanche. Mrs. Wilson stepped out of her office at that moment and apparently read the puzzlement on his face.

"Generator," she said. "Grady, our handyman, apparently just got it going. The generator runs on propane. We have a thousand-gallon tank of it."

"You'll probably need all of it," Tully said. "It's going to take a while for the highway department to get that road cleared out again."

"No doubt," she said.

"I'm sorry I haven't been able to get out and look for your husband. We'll get a search going first thing in the morning."

"I understand, Sheriff. Nothing can be done this late at night. I should have called you earlier. It's just that I put it off until I realized that even Mike couldn't be this angry, or this stupid, to be gone so long this time of year."

"Right," Tully said. He remembered her dismissing any possibility that Mike might have gone off on an affair. It had to be pretty humiliating to be married to a woman who couldn't imagine you having an affair. Even Tully's devoted Ginger had kept a wary eye on him.

Mrs. Wilson said, "I forgot to tell you that your

associate arrived earlier. He's back by the windows. I've had your drink put at his table, and your dinner will be there shortly. Hope you like pot roast."

"One of my favorites," Tully said. He thanked her again for repairing his knees and walked with her on through the lounge. He noticed five young men seated in a circle of easy chairs and a sofa. Marcus was one of them. A husky fellow in a letterman's jacket appeared to have been a participant in some recent fisticuffs. His eyes were blackened, his lips swollen and cut, and his nose solidly punched.

"Who are those chaps?" he asked Mrs. Wilson.

She glanced over her shoulder. "Oh, they're fraternity boys from Washington State University. They apparently see themselves as extreme-sport practitioners. They spent the day out cross-country skiing. I think they intended to climb Mount Blight but gave up on that after one day. According to DeWayne, my bartender, they were seated there when a gentleman in Indian attire came in and one of them started teasing him. Apparently, the man invited the boys out to the parking lot and their disagreement was settled there. That sort of thing, I should mention, is not unusual here. Our clientele for the most part are fairly physical types, if you know what I mean. Skiers, mountain climbers. We don't have DeWayne interfere too much when they get into their little disputes."

"Indian attire?" Tully said.

"Yes, your friend, I believe. He doesn't seem to be injured in any way."

"I suspect not," Tully said. He thanked her again,

excused himself, walked over to Dave Perkins's table, and sat down across from him.

Dave had his head tilted down, studying a glass of whiskey. He and Tully had been friends since childhood, often playing cowboys and Indians when they were very young. Dave had always wanted to be the Indian. He looked up. "Bo! Good to see you. Hope you didn't run into any trouble on the way up."

"Only an avalanche. And a couple of naked people. How about you?"

"Nothing of interest."

"So you didn't have anything to do with that blood out in the parking lot?"

"Oh, you noticed that, did you? I had to teach a frat boy a little respect for his elders. I'm kind of sorry now that I turned the whole tribe loose on him."

"My recollection is you're the only person in your tribe."

As far as Tully knew, the reservation and casino were part of an elaborate running joke. But he couldn't be sure. You never could be sure about Dave. With a totally insane mother and an absent father, he had suffered through one of the worst childhoods imaginable, without it ever seeming to affect his high spirits. After eighth grade, he dropped out of school and went to work in the mines. He joined the army as a sniper and scout as soon as he was old enough. The army educated him through high school and college and an MBA, and he eventually worked in army intelligence. And possibly for some other intelligence agencies. Dave never talked much about that part of his life.

"That's true," he said. "So far my tribe has only one member. But you didn't bring me all the way up here to ridicule the size of my tribe. There really was an avalanche, hunh? Bad?"

"Really bad. Wiped out the road, almost took out the Explorer and dammed up the West Branch for good measure. Don't know if the water will back up this far. Took out a cabin down below, though. I just barely managed to get a couple of kids out of it."

"That one of them?" Dave said, nodding toward another table.

Lindsay was eating dinner with Pap and in animated conversation with him. Pap seemed interested but a bit overwhelmed.

"That's Lindsay, all right," Tully said. "Pap looks as if he might need rescuing, but I think I'll leave him to his fate."

"You're leaving a young girl with Pap?"

"Ordinarily I wouldn't, but I think Lindsay can take care of herself."

Dave said, "When you get time, I want to hear the naked part. She's a cute little thing. Love that red hair. Must have been pretty wild."

Tully nodded at the glass of whiskey in front of Dave. "That mine?"

"I reckon. I've already had two, waiting for you to show up. So I haven't drunk much of yours. What's the deal on Mike Wilson? He still gone?"

"Yup. From what I hear, he seems to be a bit of a jerk."

Dave nodded his head. "Yeah, if he's the Mike

Wilson I know. He almost made the Olympic biathlon team twenty-five years or so ago and never let anybody forget it. The guy was a major athlete, though. I personally couldn't stomach him, but he kept himself in terrific shape."

"Sounds like he would know his way around in the snow."

"He knows the mountains in this area like I know my reservation."

"Not the kind of guy who would get lost around here, I take it."

"You take it right," Dave said. "In my opinion, Mike Wilson is not the kind of guy to disappear unless he wants to disappear."

Tully took a sip of Scotch. "You think he has a bit on the side."

"I wouldn't be surprised. Women seem crazy about him, at least until they get to know him. That was some years ago, though. I haven't seen him in quite a while."

"His wife dismissed that possibility with a laugh."

"That's kind of mean, isn't it?"

"That's what I thought."

Mrs. Wilson came up to their table. "I'm sorry to bother you, Sheriff, but there's a lady who would like to talk to you. She's up here from Boise practicing with her dog team for a race we are supposed to have next week. She's been over all the trails with her team the last couple of days. She might be able to suggest something."

"No problem," Tully said. "I'll be back in a minute, Dave."

"Can I drink the rest of your whiskey?"

"Have at it."

Tully followed Mrs. Wilson over to a nearby table. The lady was blond and slim with a pretty, nicely tanned face. She stood up as they approached.

"Janice Duffy, this is Sheriff Bo Tully."

"Pleased to meet you, Sheriff," Janice Duffy said, holding out her hand.

Tully took her hand and gave it a little squeeze.

Mrs. Wilson excused herself and went to attend to some other guests.

Janice Duffy smiled at him. "Would you mind stepping out on the veranda with me for a minute, Sheriff? It's so stuffy in here."

"It is that," Tully said. He opened the door to the veranda and they stepped out into the snow. Janice Duffy grabbed him around the neck and kissed him hard on the lips. Not being a fool, Tully kissed her back. Then he gently pushed her away.

"So," he said, "the marriage with Tom isn't working out?"

"Sure," she said, laughing. "It's working out. Tom still buys my dog food, like a truckload every month. I'm just happy to see you."

"I must say you have a nice way of showing it."

"I can be a whole lot nicer, Bo. I'm here all alone and I have a very private room. You might want to stop by later in the evening."

"Odd you should suggest that. And here I just assured my mother that I never sleep with married ladies."

"Shoot! And here I thought you might have changed," she said, pretending to pout.

The years had treated Janice well. Or maybe it was the sled-dog racing. She was lean and firm and fairly radiated health. She had married Tom Duffy while the three of them were still in college. Loud and funny and smart, she had chosen Tom for his good looks and money, instead of Tully, for love and poverty. Women were hard to figure.

"I admit it's tempting," Tully told her. "Alas, I still have my principle—I try not to do things that might cause hurt to my friends, and Tom's a friend of mine. But I do have a favor to ask."

"Really?" she said.

8

THE NEXT MORNING TULLY PUT on his long underwear, black
wool pants, checked wool shirt, wool socks, and insulated boots. Then he went downstairs and ate breakfast
with Pap and Lindsay. Lindsay immediately burst into
intense conversation with Pap, who gave Tully one of
his calm, innocent looks.

"Listen, Lindsay," Tully said, interrupting her chat-
ter. "I have to tell you something."

"What?"

"It's simply that your first assessment of Pap yesterday in the car was the correct one."

"What was that?"

"He's a dirty old man."

Pap burst out in a laugh.

"Hey, don't say such terrible things about him!

I really like your old man. I happen to think he's the most interesting person I've ever met."

Pap grinned at Tully, his teeth even and perfectly white, despite all the hand-rolleds he smoked.

"That's his modus operandi," Tully said. "You just remember what I told you, young lady. Now, I've got to go investigate the disappearance of a person."

Pap said, "You need some help, Bo, I'll be right here."

"Probably later. I get the feeling we may be looking for a body."

"A body!" the girl gasped.

"Sorry, Lindsay, but you'd have found out sooner or later."

He went back to his room and put on his shoulder holster and gun and his down jacket. Then he walked back downstairs and out to the parking lot. Janice Duffy was waiting for him at her huge, glistening-white pickup truck. It was parked next to a matching double-axle trailer that probably cost more than most houses. The trailer obviously had been specially designed for hauling her dogs.

"Well," she greeted him, "how does the mama's boy feel this morning?"

"Part fiery pain, part dull ache. And don't call me a mama's boy or I'll whack you up alongside the head. I still have my pride, you know."

"You're such a tough guy. Anyway, get in and we'll drive up to the dog pens."

The truck skidded sideways in the new snow, and Janice put it into four-wheel drive. "This new snow is miserable to drive in, but it's perfect for racing," she said. "The dogs love it."

"From the tracks, it looks like you've been up here already this morning," Tully said.

"Yeah, I came up at five to feed the dogs. Didn't have any good reason to stay in bed."

Tully smiled.

The dog pens covered at least an acre, with wire-fenced sections for numerous teams and several large flat-roofed doghouses in each section. Janice's dogs were sprawled on the roofs of their houses. Seeing Janice, the younger dogs began bouncing up and down and yelling, "Take me! Take me!" The older dogs lay there and watched, calm in the knowledge they would be the chosen ones. Tully sat in the pickup and watched as Janice stretched out the single towline from the sled, and then brought the older dogs out one by one and attached them to it with individual tug lines.

When they were all hooked up, Janice came over and told him, "The lead dog's name is Flag. He's a terrific leader. But these are all good, experienced sledders."

"Mmmm," Tully said, getting out of the truck. He wasn't a dog person, although he did appreciate a good hunting dog, as long as it belonged to someone else. "They're pretty," he said, not meaning it. "All Siberian huskies, I take it."

"Right. I can see your enthusiasm for dogs is about equal to Tom's. Still, he doesn't complain about the cost of feeding them."

"Good thing Tom is rich. This looks like an expensive hobby."

"It isn't a hobby! It's a passion!"

"Sorry," Tully said. "Anyway, Mrs. Wilson gave me a map of the lodge grounds. The so-called Pout House is about a mile upstream. Let's take a look around there first." He sat down on the sled, his back against the uprights, and took a firm grip on the handrails.

"Mush!" yelled Janice, standing on the backs of the runners and gripping the handles. She didn't crack a long whip over the dogs, as Tully had hoped.

The dogs took off with such force that Tully was nearly thrown out of the sled. He was surprised by their power. Snow sprayed in his face. Ahead of him was a surging line of fluffy tails. Not a great view, actually.

"So you really do say 'Mush'!" he yelled back at her.

"Shut up!" she said. She was riding on the backs of the sled runners.

"What do I yell to get the dogs to stop, in the off chance you fall off?"

"Shut up! I have to concentrate!"

They arrived at the Pout House much quicker than Tully had anticipated. He had been looking forward to what he expected would be a much more leisurely ride.

"Whoa!" yelled Janice. The dogs slowed to a stop, as she braked the sled, apparently to keep it from running over the dogs.

"Whew!" Tully said, pushing himself up. "That was—exhilarating."

"You really are a mama's boy, aren't you?"

"Perhaps. Now that you mention it."

He walked over to the cabin and tried the door. It

wasn't locked. He pushed it open, stamped the snow off his boots, and went inside. The cabin consisted of two rooms. A propane lantern hung from a chain attached to the ceiling. A barrel stove provided for heat and any cooking that needed to be done. A teakettle sat in the middle of the stove's flat top, which had obviously been cut and welded with a torch. He looked in the second room, which contained a bed piled with blankets and a comforter. A small bookcase contained a selection of worn paperbacks. Another lantern sat on an upturned apple box next to the bed. There was no indication the cabin had been used for some time. He took the lid off the teakettle and stuck a finger in. The water was frozen. He noticed some snow on the floor. Clearly there hadn't been heat in the room anytime recently. A second door opened to the back of the cabin. Tully pulled it open. A snowy field spread out before him. He could make out odd shapes scattered about the field and barely protruding above the snow. Then he saw the boot tracks. They led away from the cabin in the direction of the river. He closed the door. He walked back through the cabin and went out the front door.

"You find what you were looking for?" Janice asked.

"I don't know what I'm looking for, and whatever it was I didn't find it. A vehicle of some kind has mashed down the snow right up to the cabin and wiped out any tracks that might have led into it from the front."

"Wow, you detect the obvious right off," Janice said. "No wonder you have the reputation of being some kind of genius when it comes to solving crimes."

"I'll tell you what it is. I don't have a wife, so I don't have anyone to explain the obvious to."

"Wives already know the obvious."

"Yes, but good wives pretend they don't. See, Janice, that is your shortcoming as a woman. You never let men get away with explaining the obvious."

"I'll try to live with it."

Tully told her he had one more place he would like her to haul him.

"Where's that?"

"The top of the ridge behind the lodge. There's something the genius in me wants to investigate, namely if my cell phone will work from up there. It certainly doesn't work down here."

"Anything else?"

"I'll let you know as soon as I know."

9

NEXT TO A LARGE SHED, a tall, dark-haired man in striped coveralls appeared to be doing some maintenance work on a strange-looking vehicle, an orange metal cab mounted over two sets of broad rubber tracks, each set appearing to swivel independent of the other set. It was obviously used for traveling on snow. Tully told Janice to drop him off by the shed, that he would meet her back at the lodge. The man looked up as Tully approached. He put something in his mouth, chewed on it, then blew out a mouthful of husks.

"You must be Grady," Tully said.

"Yes sir, what can I do for you?"

"I'm Blight County Sheriff Bo Tully. Some of my people and I are up here investigating the disappearance of Mike Wilson. You got any idea where he might be?"

"No sir, can't say that I do. Not like Mike to just

up and disappear like that. Not without taking a car, anyway. I've already checked all the places I thought he might be. Did that before Mrs. Wilson called you."

"How about the Pout House?"

"Yes sir, drove Bessie up there this morning. I yelled Mike's name and pounded on the Pout House door and got no answer. Then I opened the door and looked in, but it was obvious nobody had been there."

"You happen to check the back side of the Pout House?"

"No sir. Didn't see any reason to. It was obvious nobody had been there." He shook a sunflower seed out of a paper bag and popped it in his mouth.

"What kind of a machine is Bessie?"

Grady cracked the seed with his teeth and blew the husks out the side of his mouth "She's a Sno-Cat, Sheriff. Use her to groom the ski trails and to get around on the property in winter."

"That's what I thought. Are you the only one who drives it?"

"Yes sir, mostly. Once in a while, Mike drives it, but not often. He prefers to get around on his skis. He's a terrific skier. But here's kind of an odd thing. Last Sunday I went into Blight City to get a case of motor oil and some other stuff—that's the morning Mike disappeared—and when I got back Bessie wasn't where I last parked her. I asked Mrs. Wilson about it, and she said she was pretty sure no one had used it. Well, a little later, when I was out looking for Mike, I could see where he had run Bessie way off down the ridge."

"That the ridge runs along above the road?"

"Yes sir. I figured Mike had to do it, but there's nothing much out there. No reason I could see to run the Sno-Cat along a ridge nobody ever goes out on."

Tully tugged on the corner of his mustache as he stared up at the mountain, now glistening white in the morning sun. "Let me see if I've got this straight, Grady. Mike Wilson left the lodge early Sunday morning. You drove into town to get some stuff Sunday and when you got back, the Sno-Cat had been moved, right?"

"Yes sir."

"And the only person who might have moved it was Mike?"

"Yes sir, as far as I know. Mike didn't like anybody borrowing equipment. We have a bunch of skis and stuff we rent out, but he wouldn't want nobody fooling with Bessie."

"And Mike hasn't been seen by anybody here since before Bessie was moved."

"Yes sir, that's it, far as I know."

"One more thing, Grady. When Mike disappears with a car, how long is he usually gone?"

"Oh, sometimes a couple of weeks. He had a development deal going for a while, some kind of housing project near Blight City. When he was working on that, he'd stay in town for weeks at a time. Without a car, though, he's got to be around here someplace. I figure something must have happened to him. If it did, he's got to be dead. No two ways about it, a man can't survive up here without shelter in the middle of winter."

"I appreciate the information. One other thing. I

notice the river here is pretty normal. Did the avalanche dam the water up this far?"

"Yes sir, went clear past here. Rose up pretty high. Lifted the dock near to the top of its pilings. I could tell this morning by the water marks and scrape marks on the pilings. The dock's got steel rings that slide up and down the pilings. The lodge has a boat tied up down there but it's a good thing it was tied to the dock and not the piling. Otherwise it would have been sucked under for sure. I never heard anything about the river being dammed up until this morning. I guess the dam must have busted loose sometime during the night, because the river was back to normal when I got up. First time anything like that has happened up here, the river getting plugged up by an avalanche. Lived here almost five years and never seen anything like it. Maybe it's that global warming thing."

"I wouldn't be surprised. Anyway, I've got a favor to ask. I brought a tracker with me, and I wonder if you and Bessie could take him out to the Pout House."

"Yes sir, that the Indian?"

"Yeah, the Indian. By the way, Grady, when did you give up smoking?"

"About a week ago. How did you know?"

"Sunflower seeds. Used them myself when I gave it up."

"Seems like once most everybody smoked. Folks knew it was bad for their health too but didn't seem to worry about it. I guess when I was little there were so many things to die from, smoking just didn't make the grade. I tell you, Sheriff, I loved to smoke, and I'm getting mighty sick of sunflower seeds."

"Know what you mean, Grady, know what you mean. By the way, I understand Mike is a terrific skier."

"Yes sir, he is that."

"So do you know if his skis are missing?"

Grady laughed. "He must have a dozen pairs, maybe more. Boots and ski poles, too. I never paid much attention to any of his ski stuff. Be hard to tell if any of it is missing. He kept most of it in the equipment-rental room if you want to take a look."

"Maybe later."

Grady cracked another sunflower seed with his teeth and blew out the husks.

One of these days, Tully thought, they'll find out that sunflower seeds cause cancer.

10

TULLY FOUND DAVE PERKINS IN the lounge talking to Pap.
They were seated on facing couches with their feet up
on the same ottoman. There was no sign of the frat
boys, but other guests wandered about looking bored.

"About time I put the two of you to work," he told
them.

"We were just talking about going down and soaking ourselves in one of the hot tubs," Dave said.

"But since neither one of us brought a swimsuit,"
Pap put in, "we was wondering if it would be all right
to go in naked."

"Fine with me," Tully said. "As long as I don't have
to see it. First, though, I've got a job for the two of
you. I just got back from the Pout House and noticed a
set of tracks leading from the back door down toward
the river. I want the two of you to go out there and

follow those tracks and see if you can make out anything from them. The Sno-Cat they use for grooming trails has wiped out any sign of tracks on this side of the cabin, so don't bother looking for those. Grady, the handyman, will haul you out there in the Sno-Cat. As for me, I've got a dog team and its driver waiting for me and I think the driver may be getting a little impatient with me."

"Impatient for what?" Pap said.

"Remains to be seen."

Tully walked out of the lodge just as a heavyset, gray-haired woman came by riding a snowmobile. She pulled up and stopped. "Howdy," she said.

Tully smiled at her. "Howdy."

"You must be the sheriff."

"That be I," he said. "Bo Tully. What's your name?"

"Marge Honeycut." She pulled the makings out of a pocket inside her jacket and began rolling herself a cigarette. "Bet you've never seen anybody do this before," she said.

"Matter of fact I have. You'll have to meet my old man, Marge. He still rolls his own."

She snapped a thumbnail across the head of a kitchen match and lit her cigarette. Bo shuddered. Pap lit kitchen matches the same way. Tully had tried it once and caught a piece of flaming sulfur under his thumbnail. Onlookers in the bar thought he had invented some new kind of wild dance.

"Sounds like my kind of man," Marge said. "I been looking for a good one."

"I wouldn't recommend him, if you're looking for a good one. A good man is hard to find these days, Marge."

"You're telling me!"

"So you work here, do you?"

"Yeah, off and on. I clean the cabins up on the mountain. Got this dogsled race coming up and some racer may want to rent Cabin Three. Cabins One and Two are buried in snow. Mostly it's all pretty easy, except for the squirrels."

"The squirrels?"

"Oh yeah, they get in the cabins and make an awful mess. I was down with a cold a couple days last week, so I cleaned Cabin Three on Sunday. I suspected the squirrels would be up to no good, so I went back up there on Monday, late yesterday afternoon, and sure enough, some of the little beggars had made a big mess. Chewed up something all over the floor. Took me near an hour to get it all cleaned up. Course I don't move as fast as I once did. I been thinking of taking a .22 up there and plinking myself a squirrel or two. They ain't fit to eat, but I might boil them up for my cat."

"Where do you live, Marge?"

"I got myself a little shack overlooking the meadow. Pretty nice place. It's lodge property, but Blanche don't charge me nothing to stay there and I do a little work for her. If Mike had his way, though, he'd probably run me off."

"People around here don't seem too fond of Mike."

Marge agreed with that assessment, referring to the owner as an anatomical obscenity.

"I see you have your own snowmobile," Tully said. "Wish I'd had the good sense to bring one with me."

"It ain't mine," Marge said. "Belongs to the lodge. It's the only snowmobile allowed on the property. Anybody shows up with one, they get run off. Grady, that's the handyman, or so they call him, he gets to use the Sno-Cat to groom the trails and do a few chores around. As far as I can see, he don't do much. Well, I'd better get to work. Nice meeting you, Sheriff."

"Likewise, Marge."

He checked his watch. Janice could wait a bit longer. He crossed the road and walked down to the river. A black, inflatable boat about twenty feet long bobbed up and down next to the dock. It was covered with a blue plastic tarp. Two large outboard motors were attached to the stern. Tully suspected they were both jets, because props would get torn up in a river. The river drifted upstream in a placid back eddy around the dock. Out twenty feet or so the current swept along with considerable force. Upstream, a footbridge suspended from large cables spanned the river. On the far side of the river, several young men raced snowmobiles furiously back and forth along the bank. Got to be locals, he thought. He wondered if one of them might be the naked person DeWayne had thrown down the front steps of the lodge.

11

THE DOG TEAM SPRAWLED ALONG its towline, most of its members asleep or yawning. Their driver sat on the sled, her chin resting on her gloved hands.

"About time you got back!"

"I had to get some of my troops activated. Now do you think your mutts can get me to the top of that ridge up there?" He pointed.

"They would love to. But don't call them mutts. They have feelings too, you know."

"Sorry."

Tully climbed aboard the sled and got a good grip on both sides. Janice yelled, "Mush!" The dogs took off in a spray of snow and tails. They reached the top of the ridge much faster than Tully had even imagined, the dogs scarcely breathing hard.

"Can you run me down the ridge now?" he asked.

"How far?"

"Several miles. I'd like to look at the avalanche from the top side."

"Mush!"

Tully pulled his stocking cap down over his ears, crossed his legs, and rested his head on the back of the sled. The runners sizzled through the snow. The mountains around were achingly beautiful. Far down below he could see the black line of the river wending its way through the canyon. He could even make out some of his favorite fishing holes, as well as the campsite of his and Susan's aborted tryst. He thought he should put up a marker. Maybe in a year or two he would think of the proper wording. He was still pondering the words for the marker when they reached the avalanche site. Susan shouted "Whoa!" and jammed down the brake. She then put down the snow hooks to keep the dogs from running off with the sled. He pushed himself up and walked over to the edge of the ridge. The slope had been scraped nearly bare by the rush of snow, ice, trees, and rocks. Several minutes passed before he found what he was looking for, a line of gray spots that ran across in a line a hundred feet or so down from the top of the ridge. Tully tugged on the corner of his mustache as he studied the spots. He walked back to the sled and sat down on it.

"Home, James."

"We're not moving an inch until you tell me what you found out."

"Just the ordinary," he said.

"And that is?"

"I think somebody might have tried to kill me. And maybe Pap, too, for good measure."

"Not again!"

"Afraid so."

"How can you tell?"

"You see those gray spots down there in the snow? I'm pretty sure somebody laid out a line of ditching dynamite. The concussion from one stick sets off all the others."

"Why in heaven's name would someone want to kill you?"

Tully laughed. There are plenty of reasons. "The real question is how did they know we would be coming along that road when we did?"

"Maybe it was just a coincidence you happened along at just the right time. You ever hear that coincidence confounds reason?" She sat down on the sled next to him. The dogs, sprawled out along the towline, turned and looked back, apparently wondering what the next move was.

"Even if you won't sleep with me," she said, "I hate to think about somebody trying to kill you."

He put his arm around her and gave her a hug. "Well, while we're up here, I better check in with the office and make sure things aren't falling apart there." He pulled his cell phone out of his jacket and dialed.

Daisy answered. "Boss! We were worried sick waiting for you to call. You might have been buried in that avalanche!"

"Almost was. Pap said if it had led us a bit more it would have. Smashed up the Explorer pretty good but didn't hurt us."

"We've got some news here, too. I'll let Herb tell you."

Herb Eliot came on. "Bo! Man, are we ever glad to hear from you!"

"How come? Somebody steal the town?"

"Not quite. But somebody murdered Horace Baker last night."

Tully sat in silence for a moment.

"You there, Bo?" Herb asked.

"Yeah, I'm here. I'm getting a bit overloaded, though. How do you know Horace was murdered?"

"He was shot in the back of the head!"

"That's a pretty good indication. Who found him?"

"His secretary, Irene Pooley."

Janice put her hand on Tully's arm. "Stop tugging on your mustache like that. You'll pull it out."

Tully put his hand in his lap.

Herb went on. "He's still in his office. We left him just like she found him, waiting for you to get back."

"It'll be a while before I get back. The road's blocked by the avalanche. Besides, we still need to find out what's happened to Mike Wilson."

"I was saving the kicker for last," Herb said.

"And the kicker is?"

"Mike Wilson is Horace's partner in that development deal."

"The one the county turned down?"

"Yeah," Herb said. "You remember Horace threatened he was going to put in a giant pig farm on the land instead? A thousand pigs! So right there we have a couple hundred people wanting to kill him, the neighbors to the pig farm, for example, some of them very capable of doing it. Anyway, his secretary, Irene, says Horace was meeting somebody in his office later that night."

"Who?"

"She said Horace didn't say who, and she didn't want to ask. He had apparently told her numerous times that if he wanted her to know something he would tell her. Irene is pretty shaken up by the whole thing. Guess she liked the miserable old devil quite a bit despite everything."

"He doesn't have any family that I can recall. Irene is about it."

Tully began to sense his rear freezing to the sled. He stood up and began stomping his feet. "Anything at the scene that might give you a clue to the killer?"

"Just that Horace had poured a glass of whiskey for someone. It was sitting across the desk from him, apparently untouched. So he obviously knew the person, knew he drank whiskey. Or she did, as the case may be."

"And he was shot in the back of the head, while seated at his desk?" Tully said. "I didn't know Horace well but I know he wasn't the kind of man to let one of his enemies get behind him. I'm slowly freezing to death up here, Herb. I've got to go. Get Lurch and Susan Parker over there to investigate the scene. See if

Susan can pinpoint the time of death. I'll be in touch later today."

"With me or Susan?"

"You."

"Right, boss. Now I've saved the really bad news for last."

"What?"

"Clarence is back!"

"Clarence! Nooo!"

"Yup. He's been gone over a month and I know everybody was hoping he'd been shot or run over or something."

"We can't have idiots shooting at him in the city."

"Couple have already tried and missed. We confiscated their rifles. They said how come, for shooting at Clarence? I said no, for *missing*!"

"I don't want any shooting in the city. Someone will get killed. You catch somebody shooting, throw him in the slammer. I know what we'll do with Clarence if we catch him again. The last time we tried to keep him in the Playpen, he scaled the chain-link fence and wiggled through a coil of concertina wire. What's he been up to this time?"

"Just the usual. He hides under people's cars and sneaks out and bites them on the ankles."

"Well, stay after him. And, Herb."

"Yeah?"

"I don't want to hear any more of your problems." He pushed the off button on the phone.

Janice was leaning into him, her head against his chest. She felt warm and surprisingly soft. That was one of the things he liked best in women, their softness. He caught himself thinking that Tom Duffy had never really been that good of a friend.

"So who's Clarence?" she said into his chest.

"A little brown-and-white dog." He gave Janice a hug. "Would you mind if we ran down the ridge as far as it's groomed? Shouldn't be much more than a couple of miles. There's no reason for skiers to come out here, so I'd like to see if there's some reason to be grooming the ridge."

A mile or so later, they came to the place where the Sno-Cat had turned around. No reason was evident for the Sno-Cat to have been driven down the ridge. They turned around.

"Maybe the person was out for a Sunday drive," Janice said.

"Could be," Tully said. "Now if you don't mind, I'd like to make one more detour."

He had Janice stop at Cabins One and Two but found nothing of interest there. Then she stopped at Cabin Three. It was several hundred feet up a trail that led back into the woods from the groomed area. "I'll only be a minute," he told her. "Might as well check it out, while we're here."

Janice sat down on the sled, her chin in her hands. Tully pushed open the cabin door. He looked up. The ceiling was open to the rafters. A piece of plywood had been laid across two of the rafters. He dragged over a chair from the table and climbed up on it. Then, with considerable grunting, he pulled himself up to the rafters until he could see on top of the ply-wood. Nothing.

He got down off the chair and searched the bed-room. He found nothing there. Then he went out the back door to the privy. It had a quarter-moon hole cut in the door. He turned the latch and went inside. There was no evident place to hide anything there. He climbed up on the bench for the toilet seats and looked for any nook or cranny where an object might be concealed. Nothing. He got down and started out. The latch had slipped down over the door. He took out his pocket comb, shoved it through the crack at the edge of the door, and pushed the latch back up. On his way back to the cabin, he even stopped and looked in a bird feeder. Not even any bird seed in it. For some unknown reason, he had begun to feel extremely uneasy. He walked through the cabin and out the front door and started up the walk. Suddenly he detected a movement off to his right. He spun and crouched, the Colt .45 coming off his shoulder holster.

"Get down!" he yelled at Janice.

She threw herself flat on the sled. The dogs had leaped to their feet. "Whoa!" she yelled at them.

He had the gun leveled at the unseen menace.

A large black shape flapped off through the trees. A raven. He couldn't remember having drawn on a bird before. Something about the missing man and the murder in town was starting to get to him. He swept the gun back and forth, watching for any movement in the trees. He saw nothing. Slowly he stood up and put the Colt back in its holster. Slightly embarrassed, he walked over to the sled. "I'm sorry," he said. "I felt something. Guess I'm getting way too jumpy."

"I felt it, too," Janice said.

"Let's mush back to the lodge. I'll buy you lunch, if you don't mind the company of a couple old geezers."

"You're not so old."

"I was referring to Pap and Dave."

She laughed.

12

THEY ARRIVED BACK AT THE lodge shortly before lunch. While Janice returned her dogs to their pen, Tully stopped by the office to inform Mrs. Wilson that so far he hadn't found any sign of her husband. He didn't mention anything about his suspicion that the avalanche had been deliberately set off to kill him and Pap. He would tell her later. Maybe she already knew. He then went up to his room, took off all his clothes, ran a tub of hot water, and lay on his back in the tub with his knees bent up, so as not to get the bandages wet. He thought it might be okay to remove the bandages but at the moment wasn't up to any unnecessary pain. He studied his stomach. It was fairly flat, at least while he lay on his back. That pleased him. He worked the faucet with the big toe of his right foot, keeping the water as hot as he could stand it. Grady, he thought, must be running the powerful generator almost full-time, to keep the water hot for the guests. On the other hand, maybe the tub water came from the hot spring. It didn't smell of sulfur, though. He got up and dressed in the clothes he had just taken off, the blue Pendleton wool shirt, the black wool hunting pants, wool socks, and insulated boots. The one exception was a two-piece set of clean silk underwear. You never knew when you might need clean underwear, particularly if you were a cop. He studied his alligator-skin boots standing next to the bed. That alligator must have been allergic to water, he thought, either that or a really cheap alligator. He went downstairs for lunch.

Most of the lunch crowd had left by the time Tully got to the dining room. The few that remained, idling over their drinks, appeared to have all been clothed by L.L. Bean. By comparison, the occupants of his own table looked a bit ratty, although no one could have been more outdoorsy than his own private dog-team driver. Janice's rough wool shirt and well-worn jeans seemed to match her tanned face and hands perfectly. Altogether, she looked pretty good to Tully, including the short bob of her curly blond hair. Dave and Pap were seated with her, and he could tell her looks weren't being wasted on either of them. He was pleased to see Lindsay at another table across the room, engaged in her usual animated conversation but now with a middle-aged couple. He was willing to sacrifice the couple. Anything to keep her away from Pap.

"I guess you've all gotten to know each other," he said, pulling out a chair.

"Oh, we've all met before," Janice said. "I've known Pap for years and had the World Famous Chicken-Fried Steak quite a few times at Dave's House of Fry."

"Yes, indeed," Dave said. "I once even escorted her and Tom around my reservation."

"That must have taken a good five minutes," Tully said, sitting down and spreading the linen napkin over his lap.

Janice laughed. "It's quite a small reservation but very nice."

"If we're done discussing our fraudulent Indian here," Pap said, "our tracker may have turned up some significant sign."

"He's right, Bo," Dave said. "Those tracks you mentioned, there's something odd about them."

"Like what?"

"First of all, there are no tracks coming back. No tracks going anywhere except to the edge of the river-bank. There's a sharp drop down to the water there, five feet or so, and the snow is all messed up like some-one fell down the bank. There's a bit of ice along the bank there and it was broken and then refrozen. A cou-ple of large rocks stick out of the bank, and it's possible a person could have slipped at the edge of the bank and hit his head on them. If he went into the river, he could have drowned."

"No sign of blood on the rocks, I take it," Tully said.

Dave shook his head. "Nope."

A waitress came over. "Would anyone like a drink?"

Tully ordered a Diet Pepsi. Pap and Dave ordered single-malt Scotches.

"What kind of pain do you two have?" Tully asked them.

"Life," Pap said.

Janice took a glass of merlot.

"So," Tully said, "you think a highly experienced outdoorsman like Mike Wilson slipped and fell into the river and drowned."

"It happens," Pap said. "A few highly experienced hunters go missing in the mountains each year."

"There's one problem," Dave said.

"It better be a good one," Tully told him.

"I weigh about one-seventy and wear a size eleven boot. Now, don't get excited, Bo, because I didn't tell her anything about what we had found, but I did ask Mrs. Wilson about Mike's shoe size and his weight. According to her, he was about the same size and weight as I am."

"So?" Tully said.

The waitress brought their drinks and stayed to take their lunch orders. All four went with the toasted cheese sandwiches and cups of tortilla soup.

"So, Dave?" Tully repeated after the waitress left.

"I very carefully walked along the tracks in the snow, step for step. First of all, there was no fresh snow in the tracks. Which means they were made after we arrived up here, because the snow stopped about nine."

"That's right," Pap put in. "It stopped just before the avalanche."

"Okay," Dave went on, "first of all, even if Mike

Wilson made the tracks, where was he all day Sunday and Monday? People were out looking and supposedly never found a trace of him. Now here's the strange part, I think. The tracks were made by boots almost the same size as mine. But the difference is that my tracks sank a good four or five inches deeper in the snow!"

"You're saying that the tracks were made by a person with the same size foot but a whole lot skinnier?"

"I would say smaller. And here's another thing. The heels of the person's boot were digging in at an odd angle, a much sharper angle than the heels of my boots." Dave stood up to demonstrate. "It looked like the person was stretching out his leg to match the longer stride of Mike Wilson. I'd bet you a World Famous Chicken-Fried Steak that the person who made those tracks was a much smaller person than Wilson."

"You don't think there's any chance Wilson could have made them?"

"I don't see how. Maybe the snow was firmer under those tracks than it was under mine but I doubt it."

The waitress brought their sandwiches and soup. "Anything else?"

Tully shook his head and she left. "Let's suppose for the sake of argument that some small person wanted to make some tracks in the snow that would appear to be Wilson's. They end at the river. How does the person get out of there without leaving more tracks?"

"Have to be by boat," Pap said, washing down a bite of his cheese sandwich with a swig of whiskey. "Or a hot-air balloon."

Tully said, "That would mean the person making the tracks had to have an accomplice."

"What's wrong with that?" Dave said.

Janice sipped her wine. "How are you going to figure out if the tracks were Wilson's or not? You would need his boots, wouldn't you?"

"Yeah," Tully said. "And if he's in the river, he'd be wearing the boots. It may be months before we find the body, maybe never, if there is a body at all. It could be all the way down to the Snake River by now."

Janice said, "Do all your lunchtime topics involve bodies?"

"You brought up the problem of the boots, Janice. I've got to preserve one of those tracks before we have another snowfall."

"How do you do that?" Pap said. "Put one of them in a freezer?"

"I don't think that would work. What I need up here is Lurch. You know what that means, Janice. Another phone call."

She responded with an exaggerated sigh.

13

FOR THIS TRIP TO THE top of the ridge, Janice hooked up a
team of the younger dogs. The new team was enthusias-
tic, to say the least, and twice almost dumped the sled.
Tully half expected to arrive at the top of the ridge slid-
ing on his belly while clinging with outstretched arms
to the back of the sled.

"Whew!" he said, getting up. "I thought I was a
goner there a few times."

"They're a peppy bunch, all right," Janice said.
"But they'll make a good team once I work them a little
more often."

Tully dug out his cell phone and dialed. A woman
answered. "Governor's office."

"I'd like to speak to the governor," Tully said. He

knew she was thinking "Wouldn't everyone?" but she said, "Who may I say is calling?"

"Blight County Sheriff Bo Tully."

"One moment, please, I'll see if he's available."

"The governor!" Janice said. "You've got to be kidding!"

The governor boomed into the phone. "Bo, how are you!"

Tully held the phone up so Janice could hear. "I'm great, Guv. How are you?"

"Fair to middling, fair to middling. I'd be a lot better if I was up hunting quail with you."

"Me too," Tully said. "But I've got a favor to ask."

He explained about the missing man and the avalanche and his need for Lurch. "So do you suppose you could have one of your National Guard helicopters haul him up to the West Branch Lodge?"

"Good as done, Bo. He'll be up there in an hour. The chopper can land in that meadow next to the lodge. I've landed there a few times myself. Give me a call when you get that mess straightened out."

"Will do, Guv. Thanks." He pushed the off button.

"Well!" Janice said. "I've never before known anyone who could pick up the phone and call the governor. And have him answer! Don't tell me he owes you a political favor."

"Naw, politics don't count for much around here. The guv's a hunting buddy, and I know the best quail hunting in the state."

"That explains it!"

Tully phoned the office. Daisy answered, "Sheriff's Department."

"Hi, Daisy. What's happening?"

"Oh, Bo! It's so good to hear from you so soon. When are you coming back?"

Tully had long ago guessed that Daisy was madly in love with him, even though both of them tried not to let on, particularly now that she was in the middle of a divorce from Albert the Awful.

"Yeah, I hate being stuck here, but we still haven't found Mike Wilson dead or alive. Is Lurch around?"

"Byron just got back from Horace Baker's office. I'll put him on." Daisy never referred to Lurch by his nickname for fear of hurting his feelings. Tully couldn't care less about his feelings, and Lurch seemed to appreciate it.

"Hi, boss!"

"You find any clues, Lurch?"

"Not much. Only Mr. Baker's prints on the whiskey glasses. Weapon was probably a .22 pistol. One shot to the back of the head. No exit wound. Looks like a professional hit. The bullet ricochets around inside the skull and does a lot of bad stuff to the brain."

"Old Man Baker would never let somebody he didn't know get behind him," Tully said. "I doubt he ever knew a hit man. The killer must be somebody he knew pretty well. Anyway, Lurch, I need you up here pronto. Along with your usual kit of potions and the like, bring something that will let you take impressions of boot prints in the snow."

"I thought the avalanche had closed the road."

"It has. A helicopter will pick you up at the Air National Guard station in about half an hour. Be there."

"But you know I'm terrified of flying!"

"What's your point, Lurch?"

14

JANICE DROPPED HIM OFF AT the maintenance shed, then took the rowdy pups back to their pen. Tully looked around the shed for Grady Brister and finally found him in an enclosed workshop at one end of the building. Grady had something in a vise and was pounding on it with a ball-peen hammer.

"I didn't know you also worked on delicate machinery, Grady."

The handyman blew out some sunflower-seed husks and gave the object a few more whacks. He turned around, frowning. "Oh, it's you, Sheriff. What can I do for you?"

"I've got my Crime Scene Investigations unit flying in by helicopter in a few moments. I'd like you to haul us out to the Pout House in the Sno-Cat."

"Yes sir, I could do that. But there's not a lot of room in Bessie."

"There will only be you, me, and my CSI unit, three of us altogether."

"Your CSI unit is only one person?"

"Yeah, we're a small department without that many murders. I don't count friendly killings as murders."

Grady and Tully rode the Sno-Cat out to the field next to the lodge and waited. Grady didn't seem to be much of a conversationalist, so Tully drove his hands deep into his pockets and watched the sky in silence. He heard the helicopter before he saw it, sweeping in over the mountaintop. It landed a short distance away, sending up a blizzard of snow. A pale and shaky Lurch emerged from the door, dragging his aluminum forensic trunk after him. Tully ran up to help him. The chopper's copilot came to the doorway and handed Tully a card. "The governor put us at your disposal, Sheriff. Give us a call if you need us. The number's on the card."

Tully glanced at the card. Capt. Ron Stolz, Pilot, Air National Guard and a phone number.

"Thanks," Tully shouted over the roar of the engine. "I'll do that."

He picked up one end of the trunk.

"Well, Lurch, you look as if you survived the horrors of a brief helicopter ride!"

"You're right about the horrors!" Lurch shouted back.

Tully picked up one end of the trunk, and he and Lurch carried it over to the Sno-Cat. He introduced Lurch and Grady.

"So you're the CSI unit," Grady said. "I've never met one before."

"The much-abused CSI unit," Lurch said. "Wow, this is some machine. Must be based on some kind of engineering magic."

"I don't know about that," Grady said. "But it gets us anywhere we want to go."

They climbed up into the cab. Lurch was even more impressed. Tully found any kind of technology to be basically boring. He glanced around, barely stifling a yawn. He pointed to two binocular cases hanging from a metal peg. "How come you need two sets of binoculars."

"Those are Mike's. He does a lot of birdwatching, game animals, stuff like that. The one pair are Swarovskis. They cost a fortune, like twelve hundred dollars or more. The others are Bushnell night-vision glasses."

"What kind of birds does he watch at night?"

"Beats me. He just bought them."

Ten minutes later they arrived at the Pout House. Grady remained in the Sno-Cat with the engine running, while Tully took Lurch around to the back of the cabin.

"Those tracks on the left belong to Dave Perkins," Tully told him. "Notice how they sink down deeper than the tracks on the right."

"Could be that Dave weighed more than the person who made the other tracks," Lurch said. "On the other hand, maybe the temperature warmed up and softened the snow some when Dave made his tracks."

"Did I ask you to bring logic into this? Okay, I'll try

to find out if there's been a change in the temperature. Can you make a cast of the tracks?"

"Yeah, it's tricky, but I can do it."

"That's why the county pays you the big money."

Lurch laughed. He opened his trunk and began mixing a concoction. Once he was satisfied with the consistency, he poured it into one of the tracks.

"There's still good detail here," he said. "Apparently, the temperature has gotten colder, if anything. Otherwise, we would have lost most of the detail. I assume you're thinking about matching it up with the boots of the person."

"Actually, Lurch, we don't have the person and we don't have his boots. Otherwise, we have everything we need."

"Like what?"

"Nothing."

"I hope I didn't fly up here in a helicopter for nothing."

"Easy come, easy go," Tully said.

As soon as the mixture in the track had set, Lurch pried it up, put it in a box, and they headed back to the lodge. "We'll get you a room, at least for the night, Lurch. They have a heated pool here, fed by a hot spring. I recommend you give it a try."

"I might just do that. Maybe it will undo some of the knots I got in that chopper ride."

Tully imagined the other swimmers leaping out of the pool when they saw Lurch dive in. Hey, there were certain advantages to his degree of homely. You got a swimming pool all to yourself for one thing.

15

AS TULLY AND LURCH WALKED into the lobby, the CSI unit suddenly said, "Hey, what's that?"

"What's what?"

"In that room over there. If it's what I think it is, I want to take a look at it."

They walked over to the room. It was filled almost to all four sides with a giant box about a foot high. Protruding up from the middle of the box was a pointed mound, painted blue-green and capped with white.

"Wow," Tully said. "I've seen these things before but none anywhere near this big."

"It's a three-dimensional topographical map of the whole county!" Lurch exclaimed. "This thing must have cost a fortune!"

"Not all that much," a voice behind them said. They turned to see Blanche Wilson standing there. "Three geography majors from Eastern Washington University made it as part of their senior project. The lodge furnished only the supplies. And food and lodging. They were a great bunch of kids, unlike certain college rascals I could mention." She nodded in the direction of the WSU frat boys playing cards in the lounge. "Those guys were going to scale the steep backside of Mount Blight, but I guess the weather got too much for them. They seem to prefer sitting in the lounge and arm-wrestling. And drinking. I'm going to cut off their drinking pretty soon. Their rudeness and roughhousing have pushed me to the limit. I wish you would think up something for them to do, Sheriff."

"I'll see if I can come up with something," Tully said. "I should think you would be way past your limit by now, Blanche."

She glanced around, apparently to make sure no one else was listening. Lurch seemed intent on the three-dimensional map. "I'm afraid, Sheriff Tully," she said, "you will think me about the most insensitive person you've ever met. I have tried to appear concerned about Mike, but I'm not that good of an actress. The truth is, I would just as soon he stay gone, although I don't wish him any harm. I lied to you when I told you I didn't think there was another woman. I suppose there could be a dozen other women, for all I know. It's just that I can hardly imagine another woman taking up with him. Mike is a thoroughly nasty man. Scarcely a day has gone by since we got married that he hasn't been mean to me in some way. Not physically, mind you, but just things he would say, which can be worse than physical."

"I suppose," Tully said. "By the way, do you know anything about his business arrangement with Horace Baker?"

"Only what was printed in the *Blight Bugle*. Mike never told me anything about the development or any of his other endeavors. I do know that he was very upset when the planning department turned it down."

"Like what?"

"He about went through the roof. He was practically a maniac that whole week. Then he settled down, or as much as Mike ever settles down."

Tully wondered how he should tell her. There seemed no good way, so he simply told her. "Horace Baker was murdered last night."

Blanche Wilson seemed stunned. She staggered as she stepped backward and sat down on a bench. Tully walked over and sat down next to her. "You okay?"

"I can't believe somebody would kill Horace."

"He wasn't the most beloved person in town. But we have reason to believe his killer must have known him pretty well. Apparently, Horace had poured the person a glass of whiskey and even let the person walk behind him. He was shot in the back of the head."

Blanche stared off into space. "You think Mike might have done it?"

"It's possible, I suppose. If he somehow made it to town without a car. You told me no vehicles were missing."

"That's right. Was he killed after Mike went missing?"

"I believe so. I don't know the exact time yet. Can you think of any reason your husband would want to kill Horace Baker?"

Blanche shook her head. "Not really. There were a lot of problems that resulted from the turn-down of the new development, but killing Horace wouldn't have solved any of them as far as I know."

Lurch turned and yelled over to him. "Hey, boss, come take a look at this. It's fantastic. It has about every feature of the county in three dimensions, right down to tiny cars on the streets."

"Listen, Blanche—you mind if I call you Blanche?"

She shook her head.

"We'll get this thing straightened out. I'll keep you informed about whatever we turn up. There's no point in you worrying any more than you have to."

"I appreciate that."

"By the way, Blanche, does Mike have any guns?"

She laughed. "Dozens of them! I have no idea how many."

"Do you happen to know if one of them is a .22-caliber pistol?"

"I couldn't even guess. If you want, you can come up to our living quarters and take a look for yourself. He has a couple of large cabinets crammed with guns."

"I may take you up on that."

Blanche got up and walked toward her office.

Tully let Lurch tell him about the three-dimensional map, even though Tully could see the thing for himself.

"Look, boss, they even put in the West Branch Lodge."

"Boy, that is surprising, considering that the West Branch Lodge paid for it."

Lurch obviously wasn't listening. "See, there's even

a little ski lift between the Blight Mountain Lodge and the top of Blight Mountain."

"I hate skiing," Tully said.

"Me too," said Lurch. "But you know something, Bo, we could really use one of these maps in the department. It's got every road and trail on it. You can see the whole county in a glance."

"I suppose you'd like to make the thing yourself."

"I'd love to!"

"I think maybe you've got too much time on your hands, Lurch. Maybe you need a girlfriend."

"I have a girlfriend. At least I used to have a girlfriend. You keep me so busy I haven't seen Sarah in weeks."

"Maybe you need two girlfriends, Lurch. One here and the other in Boise."

"Maybe I'll get a job in Boise."

"Not a chance. I've already told everyone there what a terrible CSI unit you are."

"I can almost believe that."

"You better believe it."

16

TULLY HEADED ACROSS THE DINING room toward the table where Perkins and Pap were seated but passed Lindsay sitting alone at a table for two. "Mind if I join you?" he asked.

"Please do, Sheriff. Say, is it all right if I call you Bo? After all, we've already been intimate."

Tully had started to spread the large linen napkin across his lap. His head jerked and he leaned across the table. "We have not been intimate, Lindsay!" he hissed.

"Of course we've been intimate!"

"Shhh! Not so loud! And we have not been intimate!"

"You carried me naked up the side of a mountain! If that's not intimate, Bo, I don't know what is."

"You weren't naked!" Tully hissed at her. "I had you wrapped up in my coat!"

"Yeah, well, my bare heinie was sticking out. It practically froze. I think it's still blue from the cold. You want to see?"

"No, I don't want to see!"

Lindsay grinned at him. "I'm joshing you, Bo."

"You better be! I hope you haven't told this story to anybody else, that you and I have been intimate."

"Seven or eight people is all." She laughed at his reaction. "No, only kidding." Then she turned serious. "Listen, Bo, I know you risked your life to save me. You were wonderful! Thank you, thank you, thank you. If it had been up to Marcus, I'd be dead by now."

"You're welcome. But I have to tell you, Lindsay, I would have done it for any beautiful young woman."

She laughed. "I bet you would."

The waitress came over and they ordered. Tully took the Home Fried Chicken with Mashed Potatoes and Gravy, Lindsay the Rocky Mountain Seafood Platter.

Tully said, "Listen, Lindsay, can you keep your mouth shut?"

"Sure," she said.

"Okay, I believe you. We're all kind of isolated here at the moment. And there seems to be some pretty odd stuff going on."

"Like what?"

"For one thing, I'm pretty sure somebody tried to kill Pap and me with that avalanche."

Lindsay expressed her amazement with a whispered four-letter obscenity.

Tully went on, keeping his voice low. "I'm telling you now, just in case something happens. It probably won't, but if it does I want you to know, so you can tell Herb Eliot, my undersheriff. Right now I think Mike Wilson is the culprit, that he started the avalanche in an effort to kill me. I'm not sure why."

"Geez," Lindsay said, her eyes tearing up. "I don't want anything to happen to you, Bo."

"Look, there's not much chance of anything happening. But there's this very weird stuff going on. Right now we're pretty much cut off from any immediate help. If you notice anything unusual at the lodge, let me know, okay? And if something should happen to me . . ."

"Yeah, I'll tell Herb Eliot what you told me. Bo, I like it that you trust me. And maybe someday we'll be intimate."

"Don't say that!" Tully hissed.

She gave him a wicked grin.

17

AFTER DINNER, TULLY ROUNDED UP Pap, Dave, and Lurch, and took them to his room. He informed them of his latest discovery, that the avalanche probably had been started deliberately, very likely for the purpose of wiping out him and Pap as well as isolating the lodge.

"I can understand them wanting to wipe you two out, boss," Lurch said. "Lots of people want to do that, but why isolate the lodge?"

"You want to know why?" Tully said. "Well, I don't know why. As far as killing Pap and me in the avalanche, only Mrs. Wilson knew about the time we were headed up this way. Maybe she told somebody. Somehow I think the avalanche may have something to do with the murder of Horace Baker. Mike Wilson must be involved in this. He's missing and Baker's dead, and they were both partners in that development that was shut down. Lurch, was Susan able to get at least a rough time on the death for Baker?"

"She said it had to be between eleven to midnight, calculating in all the factors."

"Okay, so let's say Wilson slipped out before the avalanche and killed Baker. Then the avalanche would keep him from getting back to the lodge. If he set off the avalanche, the road out would be blocked for him to get out. Obviously, if he turns up on this side of the avalanche, that gives him a pretty good alibi for Horace's murder. Not to mention the lack of a motive, as far as we know."

Dave said, "I don't want to inflate Bo's ego any more than it already is, but we need to consider the motive for someone trying to kill him and Pap. There has never been a single murder in Blight County since he's been sheriff that Bo hasn't solved. He's even solved quite a few by legal means, but no matter what it takes he gets them solved. So if you eliminate Bo, your chances of getting away with murder in Blight County go way up."

"That's pretty much the way I see it," Tully said.

"What about me?" Pap said. "He tried to kill me too."

"True," Dave said. "But most everybody wants to kill you. You would just be a bonus."

Pap laughed, obviously pleased. He dug out the makings from his shirt pocket and rolled himself a cigarette. He snapped a thumbnail on a kitchen match. The match burst into flame, and he lit his cigarette. Tully shuddered.

"What?" Pap said. "What are you staring at?"

"Nothing," Tully said. "Any ideas? You can see how desperate I am, to be asking you guys anything."

Dave said, "Byron got a good cast off that print in the snow. We shouldn't have any trouble matching it to Wilson's boots, if we find his boots."

"Yeah," Tully said. "If we find Wilson and if we find his boots. Maybe he made those tracks and maybe he didn't. Our Indian tracker here seems to think there's something wrong about the tracks. If somebody else made the tracks as some kind of ruse, what did that person do, swim the river? There obviously are no tracks leading back from the river."

"He would have to be picked up by a boat," Lurch said. "Either that or he drowned and floated off down the river."

"There may be some rough water between here and the Pout House," Tully said. "A person taking a boat up there might really have to know what he's doing." He tugged thoughtfully on his mustache. "If those tracks were faked, made by somebody other than Mike Wilson, then Mike Wilson is probably dead. Somebody would have gone to a lot of trouble to make us think Mike fell in the river and drowned. I'm going to see if Grady, the handyman, knows whether the lodge boat might handle the rough spots upriver. If so, maybe Lurch and I will see if we can run the boat up to where the tracks drop down into the river. That way we'll know if the person who made the tracks could be picked up by boat. You two walk in along the tracks and see if you can pick up any other signs that the tracks may have been faked. Lurch and I will meet you at the river."

"Me!" cried Lurch. "Why does it always have to be me? You know I'm terrified of boats!"

Tully said, "What's your point, Lurch?"

18

THE NEXT MORNING TULLY FOUND Grady in the lodge kitchen. He was eating breakfast. Lois Getty, the woman from the lodge office, sat across from him smoking a cigarette. Tully guessed her age at about fifty. In some ways he thought of her as an older Daisy, everything about her suggesting efficiency, her trim dark skirt and white blouse, a short, businesslike bob to her dark hair, her perfect makeup that didn't quite conceal the crinkly wrinkles around her eyes.

"Sorry to intrude," Tully said.

"Not a problem," Lois said. "Grady and I were just taking a break from the guests. If they don't get that road open soon, I'm afraid we'll have a riot on our hands. Nerves are getting a little frazzled."

"They're rich," Tully said. "They can't stand being at the mercy of anything, let alone an avalanche."

"Yes sir, you're right about that," Grady said.

Tully pulled up a chair and sat down next to Grady. At the other end of the kitchen, two middle-aged women were washing dishes. Lois called out to one of them. "Ethel, bring Sheriff Tully some coffee and a plate of that strudel."

Tully wondered how she knew he was in serious need of strudel.

She turned to Tully. "Any sign of Mike?"

Tully shook his head. "Nothing."

"Not like Mike to stay gone this long without taking a car," Grady said. "Something has happened to him. I've known him about five years but I can't say I know much about him, except he was a major athlete at one time. I guess he had a good chance at making an Olympic biathlon team years ago but hurt his leg or something in the tryouts."

"The one where they ski around in the woods and shoot at targets?"

"Yes sir, that's what I understand. He always kept himself in good shape. I have a lot of trouble believing Mike could have died because of some accident out in the woods."

One of the cooks brought Tully a cup of coffee and a plate of strudel. He thanked her and ate a piece of the strudel. It was the best thing to happen to him in days. Life is getting rough when strudel rates that high, he thought. "Well, I don't have a clue what could have happened to Wilson. But I'm not leaving until I find out."

"Good," Lois said.

"So, Grady," Tully said, "what I need right now is a boat. Can you loan me the lodge's?"

"Sure. It's a twenty-foot inflatable with outboard jet motors. Use it to take fishermen down river in the summer. Usually, we put it in storage in the winter, but Mike wanted it left in the river this year. Maybe he thought some of the guests might want to try fishing the West Branch. Got some mighty big browns in there. The big ones tend to bite only in winter."

"I know. Wish I was fishing for them right now. So you don't mind if I use the boat?"

"Nope. Guess the county will pay if you wreck it."

"Sure, the commissioners are delighted to cover all my costs. I've fished from shore up here a few times, and I know there is some pretty wicked whitewater in places."

"Yes sir, there is. I've run the boat quite a bit but I'd never go upriver. A fish isn't worth it, no matter how big."

"At least you should be able to give me a boating tip."

"Yes sir."

"And that is?"

"Don't do it!"

19

FROM THE DOCK, LURCH NOTICED the suspension footbridge that arched across the West Branch. "I've got an idea," he said. "Why don't we just go across the footbridge and walk upstream on the other side of the river."

"Naw," Tully said. "Not dangerous enough. Besides, the snow might be pretty deep over there."

"We could wear snowshoes."

"Shut up, Lurch, and put on your life jacket!"

Tully untied the tarp covering the boat, folded it, and laid it on the dock. He set an anchor on top to keep it from blowing away. Lurch finally got his life vest fastened.

"Tell me the truth, boss. The handyman said the river is nice and smooth all the way up to the Pout House, right?"

"Something like that, Lurch. I don't remember his exact words. Now get in the boat."

"I really hate boats!"

The performance of the jet motors amazed Tully. He could control the boat with surprising precision, barely touching the joystick on the steering console. Pushing the stick forward increased power, pulling it back decreased power. A slight tip of the stick to right or left turned the boat in whatever direction he chose.

"It takes a lot of experience to run one of these boats up through whitewater!" he yelled at Lurch.

The CSI unit looked back at him from the bow. "Whitewater! I've never heard whitewater described as 'nice and smooth.' How many years you been doing this, boss?"

"This is my first time. Pretty darn good for a beginner, don't you think, Lurch?"

Tully burst into laughter at the look on Lurch's face.

As the water grew increasingly violent, the boat began to twist and buck as if it were alive. As they rounded the first bend, the river seemed to rear up and curl back down toward them. Even above the roar of the water, Tully could hear Lurch's screams. They climbed a wall of water with Lurch lying sprawled halfway back from the bow, his hands clutching two straps on the floor. The bow burst through an explosion of water and then toppled forward into a deep, dark trough. Water surged through the interior of the boat and drained out the stern. For a moment, all Tully could see of Lurch were the two hands holding on to the straps. Then they were climbing another wall of water. The boat slid steadily up out of the trough and stopped atop a massive boil of whitewater. Tully managed to hold himself upright by clutching with one hand the edge of the windshield. He pushed the joystick all the way forward. The boat burst out into thundering rapids that were actually a relief from what they had gone through. Beyond the rapids, Tully made out a stretch of smooth water. Pap and Dave were standing on the bank. Lurch looked back at Tully. The Crime Scene Investigations Unit's mouth was open, as if frozen in midscream.

"Can you believe this, Lurch?" Tully shouted to his CSI unit. The roar of the rapids drowned out any reply from Lurch. Tully eased the joystick back and the boat slid into placid current next to the bank.

"How was it?" Pap called down.

"Piece a cake!"

"How come Byron's mouth is hanging open like that?" Dave said.

"First time in a boat, I guess. He'll get used to it. You fellas find anything?"

"I'm freezing!" Lurch yelled.

"Nothing," Dave said. "But I'm more convinced than ever that Mike Wilson never made these tracks."

Pap said, "I found an arrow sticking out of the snow over here. Maybe somebody killed Mike with a bow and arrow."

"What kind of point?"

"Target."

"If you're going to kill somebody with an arrow, you would at least use a hunting point," Tully said. "You probably didn't notice that that whole field is an archery course. Targets are scattered all over the place. They're half buried in the snow though."

"I'm freezing!" Lurch yelled.

Tully leaned out of the boat so he could get a closer look at the rocks. He detected no sign of a head having hit them.

"I've got an idea," Lurch said.

"What's that?"

"Let me out here and I'll go back with Dave and Pap."

"Naw, I need you to hold down the bow of the boat, Lurch. We're going farther upstream."

"Nooooo! Let Dave or Pap do it!"

"I can't do that. They're much too valuable to me. Don't you realize a person could get killed out here, Lurch?"

He shouted at Pap and Dave. "Got to go!"

He backed the boat into the current. The engine thundered and the boat slid easily around a bend and up through a lesser rapid. Ahead, Tully made out a cove where assorted logs and other driftwood had been pushed up on the shore. He headed for it.

He yelled to Lurch over the roar of the engine. "What's in the middle of that mess of driftwood?" He pointed.

Lurch turned and squinted. "Looks like some clothes! Take her in closer, boss!"

Tully ran the bow of the boat up onto the driftwood and shifted the motors into neutral.

Lurch turned and looked at him. "We got ourselves a body."

"Ten to one we've found Mike Wilson, Lurch."

"It's got rubber boots on."

"Excellent!" Tully picked up a long pole with a hook on the end. "See if you can get that hook on its belt."

After several misses, Lurch finally hooked the dead man's belt and was able to drag the corpse over to the boat.

"What do you think, Lurch?"

"Could be Wilson, all right. It doesn't look as if it's been in the water that long."

Tully got up and made his way to the bow.

"Let's see if we can drag it into the boat. Get hold of that leg and I'll grab this one."

They both heaved back and the body slid into the boat facedown.

Tully reached in the man's hip pocket and pulled out a billfold. He flipped it open. "The party we just dragged in is who we thought it might be—Mike Wilson."

"Good. Maybe we can go back now. I need to change into some dry clothes. I'm freezing."

"I myself am still fairly dry. Finding, Mike, though, pretty well screws up all my theories."

"Good!"

"But you're going back to the office, Lurch."

"How?"

"By helicopter, how do you think?"

"At least it won't be by boat!"

"Hmmm. I hadn't thought of that possibility."

Tully studied the trees on the bank above them. "You get the feeling we're being watched, Lurch?"

"I didn't want to mention it."

Upon returning to the dock, Tully sent Lurch staggering up to the lodge to get some dry clothes on and to bring back a stretcher. The trip back down had been twice as bad as the trip up but at least much faster. Tully started wrapping the body in the boat tarp. Ten minutes later Pap and Dave came down carrying a stretcher. Ski lodges always have stretchers, Tully noted. Dave snapped the stretcher open and they rolled the body onto it.

Pap watched as Tully and Dave lifted the stretcher out of the boat and set it on the dock. "I never much minded making a dead body, but I never wanted to fool with it after I'd made one. What we going to do with it now?"

"First thing," Tully said, "we'd better get Blanche Wilson down here to make a positive ID. The billfold says this is Mike Wilson. The driver's license picture looks kind of like our man here, but we need to make sure."

Flakes of snow began to drift down. "Pap, go get Mrs. Wilson, will you?"

"You got it, Bo."

"What's your plan?" Dave said.

"I'll call the chopper and get it in here as soon as I can. We'll send the body out on it, and Lurch, too, much as he hates it. Maybe I'll threaten him with another boat ride. In any case, we'll get the body back to Susan, and she'll be able to tell us the cause of death pretty quick. Probably won't get much info on time of death. Then I want to get Lurch working on his computer. He knows how to do some seriously illegal things. Maybe we can't exactly use them in court, but we can get some leads."

"I take it you don't think Mike fell in the river and drowned."

"Bodies don't float upstream, Dave, and this body was upstream of the tracks."

"Maybe the tracks aren't his. Maybe he fell in upstream of where he was found. How about that?"

"Try not to be a nuisance, Dave."

Mrs. Wilson came down to the dock. She had a green wool cape wrapped around her. The cape and her hair were speckled with snowflakes.

Tully pulled back the tarp so Mrs. Wilson could see the face of the body. She slumped as if about to faint. Dave caught her. She put her hand to her mouth.

"That's Mike," she whispered

Tully covered the body back up. "Death face-to-face is always a shock. Even if you don't know the person."

"You okay, Mrs. Wilson?" Dave said.

"Yes, thank you." She stepped forward, looking at Tully. "Is there anything else, Bo?"

"Yes, there is. I don't know if this is the time to tell you but I will anyway. I think your husband was murdered. I don't know why or how, but maybe I will soon."

"Murdered?" she said in a soft voice.

Tully nodded. "Yeah, I'm shipping the body out of here tonight by helicopter. Our medical examiner will be able to determine cause of death, I hope."

"You don't think he drowned?" she asked.

"That's certainly a possibility. We'll know soon enough."

As soon as Dave had walked Mrs. Wilson back to the lodge, Tully and Pap wrapped the blue plastic tarp around the stretcher and fastened the package with bungee cords.

The two of them then carried the body up to the utility shed.

"That Mike?" Grady asked, wiping his hands with an oily cloth.

"Yep," Tully said. "Mrs. Wilson identified him as such."

"She'll have her hands full running this place now," Grady said. "Mike could be a real pain, but he did a lot of work around here, stuff Blanche can't do."

"I hate to tell you this, Grady, but I need you to run me up to the top of the ridge in Bessie, so I can make a phone call."

"Yes sir, I figured as much. Guess the dog teams didn't work out so good."

"You got that right."

Tully wouldn't mention it to Janice, but the Sno-Cat was a lot more comfortable than the dogsled. Tully thought maybe the Sheriff's Department had serious need of such a vehicle. Sure, several of the commissioners would drop dead when he presented the idea, but new technology always results in casualties. The commissioners were only politicians anyway and easily replaced.

He called the number on the National Guard pilot's card. A female voice at the guard station told him that at that moment Stolz and his helicopter were out on a rescue mission. She would get Ron up to the lodge, she said, as soon as he returned. "Can I give you a heads-up call when he gets back?"

"Can we wait up here a bit?" Tully asked Grady.

"My time is your time," the handyman said.

"We'll await your call," he told the woman. He gave her his cell phone number.

Tully stared out at the falling snow while they waited. After a bit he said, "Where are Cabins One and Two?"

"Farther up the mountain past Cabin Three. You want to run up there?"

"Might as well."

The groomed trail wound up considerably higher on the north side of the mountain, with one ridge branching off to a higher ridge and that ridge branching off to yet another. They at last arrived at Cabin Two, which was almost buried in snow.

"Nobody stays at Cabins One and Two this time of year," Grady said. "From here the trail levels out and runs north for about five miles. Cabin One is right at the end. I haul skiers up here with the Sno-Cat and they can ski out to the end and then ski downhill all the way back to the lodge. I checked out both One and Two earlier looking for Mike, and there were no tracks leading into either one."

"It's beautiful," Tully said. "Makes me want to take up skiing."

"I prefer the Sno-Cat," Grady said.

"Well, sure," Tully said.

His phone rang. The woman said Ron Stolz was on his way.

20

THE HELICOPTER LANDED IN THE clearing next to the lodge an hour after Tully got the call from the Air Guard station. They loaded Mike Wilson's body on the chopper.

"You ready, Lurch?" Tully asked.

"Ready as I'll ever be."

"Good." He reached in a pocket and took out several folded sheets of paper. "When you get a chance, Lurch, run a check on these names for me. Find out everything you can about them."

"Anything else?"

"Yeah, an ambulance will meet you at the airport and haul the body down to Susan's lab. We should know the cause of death pretty quick. Eliot will pick you up and take you to the office, so you can get busy on your assignments."

"When am I supposed to sleep?"

"When these murders are solved. Right now, get me the info on the list. And don't tell me how. There's no point in both of us going to prison."

"Right."

"You're not going soft on me are you, Lurch?"

The CSI unit shook his head.

"Good."

The chopper lifted off in a blizzard of snow. Tully could see Lurch's pale face peering down at him from a side window.

Speaking of going soft, Tully thought, I'm exhausted. He tramped through the snow back up to the lodge and climbed the broad front steps using the handrail. Inside the entrance, he stepped into the room with the 3-D map of Blight County. He sat down on the bench against the wall. He didn't bother to turn on the room lights, enjoying for a moment the darkness and solitude. The rowdy quartet of frat boys came in through the lodge door and headed toward the bar. Marcus Tripp, Lindsay's former young friend, came trailing in a short while later. He seemed sad. Maybe he was still mourning his car.

Tully leaned his head back against the wall and studied the peak of Mount Blight protruding above the top of the box. After a moment he got up, turned on the lights, and walked over to the map. All the cross-country ski trails were marked on it, as well as the hiking trails, the ski trails in dots of white, the hiking trails in dots of green. He studied the map for a long time, then walked into the restroom. He washed his hands and face and then his hands again. There are some things that never wash off.

When he got to the dining room, most of the other guests were already at their white-clothed tables eating and drinking. It sounded as if some of them had been doing substantially more drinking than eating. He pulled out a chair and sat down with Dave and Pap.

"I guess you got Lurch into the helicopter okay," Pap said.

"Yeah, kicking and screaming. It will be good to get him back to the department, where he can do some actual work. I pulled the boots off the body, bagged them up for Lurch so he can see if there's a match between them and the impressions he made of the tracks in the snow."

"I can't imagine there will be a match," Dave said. "Wilson was as heavy as I am, maybe heavier. The tracks were made by somebody a lot lighter. I'll bet on it."

The waitress came and took Bo's order. He went with steak, mushrooms, baked potatoes, and pea salad. Dave and Pap were already eating the same. "I'll take a single-malt Scotch, too," Tully told the waitress.

"Getting pretty fancy there," Dave said.

"Treating myself," Tully said. "After today, I need a treat."

"I saw you having dinner with that other little treat," Pap said.

"Who? Lindsay? You stay away from her, Pap!"

"I think that's pretty stingy of you, wanting her all to yourself."

Dave smiled. "I'm staying out of this. Two old codgers fighting over a young girl."

"Hey, nobody's messing with that girl," Tully said.

Pap chuckled his evil chuckle. "Just joshing you, Bo, just joshing you. She does seem to have taken a liking to me, though."

Tully shook his head at the hopelessness of dealing with Pap. The waitress brought his drink. He took a sip and almost spit it out on the table. Reluctantly, he managed to swallow. "Yuck," he said, screwing up his face. "That is absolutely the worst Scotch I've ever tasted. It certainly isn't single-malt." He turned and looked over at the bar. Instead of DeWayne, one of the waitresses was pouring drinks. "How can she mess up a single-malt Scotch?"

"DeWayne must have got sick or something," Pap said.

Voices at a table in a far corner grew louder and then angry.

"Wonder what their problem is," Dave said, twisting around in his chair to see better.

"Probably ordered single-malt Scotch," Tully said, cutting into the steak on the plate the waitress had just slipped in front of him. He forked a piece into his mouth, ignoring the ruckus in the corner.

"Hey, they're jumping up and starting to go at it!" Dave said, happily.

Tully continued to chew.

Blanche Wilson came up behind him and whispered in his ear. "Bo, would you please handle that business in the corner. DeWayne isn't here right now."

Tully heaved a long sigh. "Yes, ma'am."

He shoved his chair back and tossed his napkin onto the table. He got up and started to mosey toward the three men in the corner, one of whom now threw a punch at one of the other men, missing wildly. He heard Pap tell Dave, "I taught Bo to mosey like that."

"I thought it was a fairly professional mosey," Dave said.

Tully came up to the men. "Gentlemen, gentlemen, you're disturbing the ladies, particularly the lovely ones at your own table." The young women were in fact looking extremely annoyed. One of the burlier of the fighters spun around and stuck his face in Tully's. "Beat it, pal. This ain't none of your . . ."

Tully felt the familiar numbness rising up his right arm. He didn't want to look down but he did. The man was flat on his back, a bit of blood leaking from the corner of his mouth. It often bothered Tully that he never afterward had any recollection of hitting a person. This was once again the case. It usually happened as soon as the spittle sprayed by some drunken idiot hit his face. Or maybe it was the sheer banality of tough talk. The other two fighters looked shocked. Tully reached down, grabbed the prostrate drunk by the lapels, lifted him up, and placed him in his chair. The man slumped forward, his head coming to rest in his plate. Tully took a glass of ice water from the table and dribbled some on the back of the man's neck. The man moaned and shoved himself upright. The women at the table were silent and obviously disgusted, although by no means embarrassed. Tully turned to the other two men. "So, is this little disagreement over?"

They nodded.

"Good," Tully said. "The problem is we're all trapped here together, and tempers are getting a little short. Mine is shortest of all, as you can see. So please try not to annoy me again."

One of the men said, "How come all the hassle?"

"Maybe because we've had a murder or two since you've been up here."

"There might be another," one of the men growled.

Tully turned to face him. "I want you to look over at that table on the far side of the room. Those two men standing there with their hands in their jackets? They belong to me. If one of you makes a wrong move when I turn my back, or any other time, they'll shoot you dead. So you better hope nothing happens to me anytime soon. Am I clear about that?"

The men nodded.

He looked the women over once more. They were all much younger than the men, dressed to the nines, and with hard-edged good looks. He said, "I hope I didn't disturb your dinner, ladies."

One of the blondes gave him a wink and a quick little smile. "You have a lot of nerve," she said.

When he got back to his own table, Blanche Wilson was furious with him. "When I asked you to handle the

situation, I didn't mean for you to knock people unconscious."

"I'm sorry, Blanche, I thought that's what you
meant. Besides, I knocked only one person unconscious.
If you want the other two knocked unconscious, I'll go
back and take care of it."

Blanche Wilson stomped back toward her office.

21

AT SIX THE NEXT MORNING Tully was up and seated alone at a table in the dining room, drinking his first cup of coffee of the day and waiting for his breakfast. Lindsay came up behind him and tapped him on the shoulder. Tully jumped.

"My, you're jumpy today," she said.

"Yeah, well, I guess crime is getting to me."

"May I sit with you?"

"Sure, if you promise to be good."

"I'll be good," she said. "And I have something really good to tell you. You know how you asked me to watch out for anything strange going on around here?"

"Yeah."

She told him how about midnight she couldn't sleep and decided to tie a plastic bag around her cast and go down to the basement and sit in the hot tub.

"And guess who was already sitting in it."

"I haven't a clue."

"Your dad!"

Tully uttered an anguished "Nooo!"

"Yes!"

"I hope you went back to your room instantly."

"No way. I climbed in across from him and we had a great time."

"Please don't tell me that!"

"He was a perfect gentleman, Bo. I can see you don't know your own dad very well."

"Were you wearing a swimming suit?"

"Yes, silly!"

"Was he?"

"I was afraid to look. Anyway, he told me some wonderful stories about when he was sheriff, and how much better he was than you."

"Sounds like Pap all right. So that's your big revelation, that Pap thinks he was a better sheriff than I am?"

"No, it isn't. Do you want to hear this or not?"

"Yeah, tell me."

"I headed back to my room about one-thirty and was just about to open my door at the far end of the hall . . ."

A waitress delivered Tully's bacon and eggs and hash browns, and took Lindsay's order, the fruit cup and a bran muffin. Tully poured her a cup of coffee from the thermos on the table.

"And?" he said.

"And just as I was about to close my door, I saw

a man come out of the suite of rooms at the other end."

"Somebody playing footsie, is that what you think?"

"At one-thirty in the morning? Of course that's what I think!"

"Maybe it was the woman's husband, going down for an early morning hot tub."

"Not a chance!" Lindsay leaned across the table and whispered. "Unless, of course, he has come back to life!"

Tully tugged on the corner of his mustache. "You're saying the suite of rooms belongs to the Wilsons?"

"Right! What kind of detective do you think I am?"

"A pretty good one. So, did you recognize the man?"

"No. He was in a shadow and too far away. He was tall though."

"Who do you think it might have been?"

"None of the jerks from school, that's for sure."

"How about DeWayne, the bartender? He would be my guess."

"Could be."

Tully released his mustache and drummed his fingers on the table. "The plot thickens."

Lindsay grinned at him. "So, do you want to hire me as a detective for your department?"

"Sure, fifteen hundred a month and all the graft you can collect."

22

AFTER BREAKFAST, TULLY WENT OVER to Grady's shop. The handyman apparently hadn't arrived for work yet. Tully wandered about the shop, looking at his tools. He loved tools. There were chain saws, table saws, band saws, chop saws, radial-arm saws, reciprocal saws, and even a powerful-looking saw mounted in a frame on a wall, apparently for the purpose of cutting large sheets of plywood. Sheets of pegboard contained hundreds of hand tools, each on its own black outline. Tully had not a clue about the uses for most of the tools. It was evident that Grady was equipped to handle any emergency that might befall the lodge, even to totally replacing it.

Tully opened a door at the back of the shop. A wooden walkway led to a small house behind the shop. Tully walked over and knocked. Grady opened it. As usual, he seemed pleased to see the sheriff.

"Morning!" he said. "Come on in, Mr. Tully."

"Don't mind if I do. Grady, you have a cozy little place back here, nicely screened off from all the turmoil of the lodge."

"Yes sir, it suits me fine. I'm not much for socializing."

Tully pulled out a chair and sat down across from the handyman.

"Right now, Grady, the evidence seems to suggest that Mike Wilson accidentally drowned. But I don't think so. I have a feeling he was murdered."

"Murdered?"

"Yep, murdered. I'll know soon enough. My question for you is, do you have any idea at all who might have done Mike in?"

Grady scratched his head. "Nobody comes to mind, just off hand. Mike could be pretty ornery, but I don't know if he bothered anybody so much they would want to kill him. There's some pretty rough customers back in these mountains, and I'm pretty sure Mike had dealings with them. There's one in particular, a fellow named Ben Hoot. I wouldn't put anything past him."

"Like what?"

"Murder. I think Hoot could kill a man in the morning and forget about it by noon. Among other things, he runs a still someplace back in there. He is supposed to be kind of a magician when it comes to making shine."

"A bootlegger?"

"Yes sir, that's what I've heard. You might have noticed that the lodge bar is pretty generous with its servings of whiskey."

"You mean Mike bought whiskey from this Hoot?"

"I'm not saying one way or the other. It just occurred to me that if you're looking for someone capable of murder, this Hoot might be your man."

"Listen, Grady, how do I find this Hoot fellow?"

"I don't know if it's such a good idea to go out looking for him."

"Tell me anyway."

"Yes sir. Well, you take a left turn when you get to the top of the ridge above the lodge. There's that track we groom for the cross-country skiers. You know how it winds up around the mountain to the north? Right where the track heads up the mountain, there's a trail goes up to one of the lodge's cabins. Number Three it's called."

"I've been on the trail," Tully told him. "I've been to the cabin by dog."

"Yes sir," Grady said. "You keep on that trail past the cabin. Hoot lives back in there someplace. I personally have enough sense enough not to go poking around up there, and I don't advise you to do it either, Sheriff."

"Is this Hoot crazy or what?"

"Yes sir, he's crazy. And that's about the nicest thing I've ever heard said about him."

Back at the lodge, Tully found the bartender washing up some glasses. A couple of men were already having their first drinks of the day at the far end of the bar. Tully wondered if the whiskey they were sipping had been imported from up on the mountain. DeWayne looked up.

"Sheriff! How you doing?"

"Fine, DeWayne. I've got a question or two to ask you."

"Fire away."

"You're a Scragg, raised in these parts. What can you tell me about this Hoot fellow I've heard about?"

"Ben Hoot," DeWayne said. "What do you want to know?"

"Do you think he's capable of killing a man?"

DeWayne laughed. "About as capable as he is of slapping a mosquito. You think he might have killed Mike?"

"Just a thought. I don't know if anybody killed Mike, but I'll probably find out later today."

"I doubt he killed Mike."

"Why?"

"You found the body, didn't you? If Hoot killed him, you never would have found the body. Over the years, assorted folks have gone missing around here, and no sign of them has ever turned up."

"You think Hoot did them?"

"Don't know, but he's always the prime suspect. Not that anyone would have accused him of it face-to-face. As you know, Sheriff, folks have a way of going missing in these mountains."

"I hear he has a still back in the mountains. Supposed to be some kind of magician in the manufacture of shine."

DeWayne smiled. "I hear you got a really bad Scotch last night."

"That I did."

"What kind of magic is that?"

"Maybe black magic," Tully said. "Are you telling me the girl might have got hold of the wrong bottle of booze?"

DeWayne's smile broke into a grin. "Mike liked to say that a second shot of single-malt Scotch is a waste of good whiskey. After the first shot it all tastes the same. That's what he liked to say."

"What do you know about this Hoot? You apparently think he's pretty dangerous."

"I actually don't know much about him personally. Nobody does, really. He keeps to himself and seems pretty serious about being left alone. Folks have learned not to fool with him. I know he runs a trapline in winter. He's about the last guy around here who is still trapping. Anyway, I don't think Mike was dumb enough to cross him in some way. Hoot is one scary guy."

"I'm going to pay him a little visit."

"Suit yourself, Sheriff."

23

THE SNO-CAT STOPPED AT THE intersection of the trail and the groomed ski track. Tully tossed down the snowshoes Grady had loaned him.

"You know how to use those contraptions?" the handyman asked.

"I'm an old hand at snowshoeing. You just point out the starter to me and I'll be off."

"Yes sir, that's about what I figured."

Tully slipped his boots into the harnesses and fastened them. "How far in to Hoot's cabin you reckon?"

"Don't know. Never been dumb enough to go there, Sheriff."

Tully glanced at his watch. "Well, it's ten-thirty now. How about you meeting me back here at two-thirty?"

"Yes sir, I'll be here. Hope you are."

"Me, too."

Tully plodded past Cabin Three and on up the trail. The woods seemed to close in around him as he advanced. He had never before thought of woods as creepy, but now he did. The dark, ancient trees, many of them gnarled, seemed like something out of a fairy tale, a Grimm's fairy tale. A raven flew in and landed on a branch a short distance away. It cocked its head and examined him, as if he were some strange, unknown creature. Tully almost expected the bird to speak. Then it flew off silently, except for the flapping of its wings. He wondered if maybe it were flying to Hoot's place to make a report. He plodded along for an hour, the woods seeming to become darker and denser at each step. Finally, off in the distance, he made out the lines of a cabin. No smoke came from its chimney.

Presently, the dogs, two large, mean-looking creatures, came for him, silent as the raven. They stopped twenty feet away, their muzzles twisted in snarls. Then they began to advance slowly.

A voice came from behind some nearby trees. "Show them your badge, Sheriff. That might put a scare into them."

Tully reached inside his jacket. "I'll show them my Colt .45 if they take two more steps."

"In that case, hold up there a second. Dogs! Back! Porch!"

The dogs seemed to shrink at the command. They backed away, then turned and slunk under the cabin porch.

The voice said. "So what brings you up this way, Bo?"

"You know my name?"

"Yup. I make it my business to know anything that might cause me trouble. I know about Pap, too. If you had been Pap I would have killed you right off. He isn't a man to fool with."

"I'm not either, Hoot! And I've got some questions for you. Maybe you want to answer them right now?"

"To tell the truth, Bo, I'm freezing out here."

Ben Hoot stepped out from behind the trees. He was barefooted and wearing only his long underwear. He had a scraggly white beard and long gray hair that streamed down his back. In one hand he held a carbine rifle. He lowered the hammer and then gestured with the rifle toward the cabin. "Come on in. I'll brew us up a pot of tea."

"Tea?" Tully said, surprised.

"Yup, tea. What did you expect, Ben Hoot to be uncivilized or something?"

Tully took his hand out of his jacket. "I didn't expect tea. What are you doing out here in the snow with no clothes on? It's noon." He slipped off the snowshoes.

"The dogs heard you coming and woke me. I was up most of the night, taking care of business."

"I never heard the dogs bark."

"They don't bark. I taught them not to. They just growl."

The dogs muttered beneath them as Tully and Hoot stepped onto the porch.

"How do you teach dogs not to bark?"

"You put your boot up alongside their heads. Works

on people too. I understand you're pretty quick with your fists. Guess that might work fine on people, but not much good on dogs."

Off to one side of the cabin, Tully noticed an open shed hung with stretchers of animal pelts. Two of the pelts he saw belonged to wolves. He could smell skunk.

The inside of the cabin was surprisingly neat, except the blankets on the single bunk seemed to have been tossed back in the manner of a man leaping out of it in a hurry. Two chairs sat next to a small table. Hoot pulled one out and indicated for Tully to sit in it. He leaned the rifle against the wall, stuffed some shavings and kindling in the stove, and lit the fire.

"How's trapping?" Tully asked him.

"Pretty good, especially now the other fellows have given it up. I spoke to them about finding other occupations. They seemed to see the sense of it right off. You have to be careful about trapping. You overdo and it takes a long while for the furs to come back. I try to be a low-impact kind of person."

"Low-impact," Tully said.

"That's a term I picked up from a magazine. I'm not an illiterate, like most of the folks around here. A nice lady by the name of Jennifer drives a library van up the West Branch Road once a month. I'm about the only person gives her any business. She comes up here mostly for me, and I appreciate it. I usually take three or four magazines and a couple of Willys.

"Willys?"

"Will Shakespeare. You're a college man, Bo. I imagine you've heard of Willy."

"I know the name."

Hoot set a copper teakettle on the stove. "Water will get hot pretty quick. Hope you like Twinings English Breakfast."

Hoot set a bowl of sugar and a spoon on the table next to Tully. "Got a can of condensed milk, if you take cream."

"No, this is fine."

"Good. The can is getting kind of clogged up around the holes. So you want to know if I killed that fellow you pulled out of the river. Nope, I didn't. I figured the time would come when I might have to do Mike, but I kept putting it off. Getting soft in my old age. And then somebody beat me to it. Never put off until tomorrow what you can do today."

"You think somebody killed him?"

"Yeah, Mike Wilson wasn't the sort of person who would jump in a river. Nor fall in one. I watched you and your helper haul his carcass into your boat."

"You know who killed him?"

"Nope. Wouldn't say if I did. The person performed a service to the community, and I wouldn't want to cause him any inconvenience for his trouble."

"You're telling me I made the trip in here for nothing?"

Hoot laughed. "Not for nothing. You're getting a nice cup of tea."

He placed four tea bags in a flowered ceramic teapot and filled the pot with boiling water. "I let it steep about three minutes. I usually estimate the time, but you have a watch."

Tully took off his wristwatch and set it on the table in front of him so he could keep track of the time.

"So you trap skunks?" Tully said.

"You smelled that one, did you? I trap about everything that's got a decent pelt. You know how to keep a skunk from spraying?"

"That bit of knowledge has somehow escaped me."

"Good, I can teach you something. You shoot them about an inch up from the bottom of the belly. That paralyses them and they can't squirt. My aim was a little off on the skunk you smelled. I'm getting old and my eyesight isn't so good. How's our time?"

"Getting close."

Hoot waited another minute and then poured the tea. Tully stirred a heaping spoonful of sugar into his and took a sip. "Perfect," he said.

"Thanks," Hoot said. "I don't get many guests. I think the last one was 1947."

Tully smiled. "Well, I appreciate your time. You've been very generous with it."

"Good. I will tell you something, though. I noticed you poking around the Wilsons' cabin the other day, the one they call Number Three. You drew down on me, if I recall correctly. I figured you were looking for something. Not much happens on this mountain I don't know about, and one night I was out very late, Monday night it was, actually well into Tuesday morning, and I see this fellow on skis. Strange to see someone out skiing in the middle of the night. There's a hollow old tamarack snag up the mountain a couple hundred yards or so from that cabin. The woodpeckers have been at the snag and pecked a good-sized opening about eight feet up. The fellow slides to a stop on his skis and tosses a package up into that opening. It was wrapped in shiny plastic. I could see the plastic shine in the moonlight. I suspect it was whatever you were looking for."

"You know what's in the package?"

"Nope, none of my business."

"You recognize the man?"

"Wouldn't say if I did."

"What time?"

"Don't know the time. The moon was out and far down in the west."

Tully drank the last of his tea and put his cup back on the table.

"You may have helped me solve this case," he said. "Thanks, Hoot."

"You're welcome. And, Bo?"

"Yeah?"

"Don't come back."

24

GRADY WAS WAITING FOR HIM in the Sno-Cat. "I see you made it out alive, Sheriff."

"Yeah, but I wouldn't advise your hotel guests to go wandering off down that trail. They might not be so lucky."

"Yes sir. You saw him then?"

"I don't want to talk about it, Grady. Let's just say I'm happy to be back."

"Yes sir." Grady started up the Sno-Cat and drove them back to the lodge.

Blanche met him at the door. "Good news, Bo."

"I can use some."

"The phone company has hooked up a temporary line. You won't have to go up on the ridge every time you want to make a call."

"Great!"

"But you'll have quite a wait. There's a long line of guests waiting to use the phone and let their families know they're okay."

"How long have you lived in Blight County, Blanche?"

She appeared puzzled. "All my life."

"Then you know there's the Blight way and no way."

He walked to the head of the line in Blanche's office and tapped the caller on the shoulder. "Hang up, partner. I've got some urgent police business."

The man looked up, a snarl starting to curl his lips. The snarl faded. It was the same man Tully had knocked unconscious the evening before.

"Got to go," he said into the phone. "I'll call you later." He hung up.

"How's the jaw?" Tully asked.

"Sore," the man said. "But not too bad."

"Good." The man went out and Tully kicked the door shut behind him. He dialed the department. Daisy answered.

"Bo! How are you?"

"Just the ordinary. I think somebody tried to kill me and Pap. Or rather tried to kill me. They would have got Pap as a bonus."

"You watch out for yourself, Bo. I don't want you killed!"

"Don't worry, sweetheart, little things like that keep me sharp. How's everything there?"

"It's a madhouse! I can't wait till you get back."

"They finally got the phone hooked up," he told

her. "I suppose it will be a couple days more before they have the road cleared enough for us to drive out. Is Lurch around?"

"Yeah. Hold on a sec!" She yelled in his ear, "Byron! Bo's on line one!"

Got to do more work on phone protocol, Tully thought.

Lurch came on. "Boss, I haven't slept in three days! There's no way I'm flying a helicopter back up there!"

"Only if I need you up here, Lurch. But right now I don't. Did you find out from Susan the time of death for Horace Baker?"

"Between eleven and midnight Monday. And I was right about the gun, too. A .22 caliber."

"How about the striations?"

"Good. We find the gun, boss, we can match it to the slug."

"Probably not much chance of that. Whoever did the killing probably deep-sixed the weapon but I may have a lead. Now, how about Mike Wilson?"

"He didn't drown. Susan says the cause of death was blunt-force trauma. She says he was hit with something on the back of the head, but it didn't break the skin. He died before he got in the river. She estimates that it took him at least an hour to die. No sign of water in either his stomach or lungs."

"So he was murdered."

"Looks that way. Dead men usually don't jump in rivers by themselves."

"How about the boots then?"

"They match the tracks in the snow."

Tully tugged on his mustache. "He could have hit his head on the rocks when he fell in the river."

"Susan says no. She says if he hit his head on those rocks, he would still have been alive when he went in the river. There would have been water in his stomach and lungs, because he would still have been breathing. And there's no sign of the kinds of gouges rocks usually make. Besides, the blow on the back of the head couldn't have been made by rocks."

"Any other injuries?"

"Yeah, his nose was broken."

"What? Like in a fight sometime?"

"No, it's freshly broken. Susan said she suspects he landed facedown when he was hit. That's what broke his nose."

"It's all very clear to me now, Lurch. Someone hit him on the head hard enough to kill him, but then he walked from the Pout House to the river but died before he hit the water."

"That's the way I see it."

"Yeah, I bet you do. Any idea of the time Wilson died?"

"Susan said because of the cold, it's too hard to tell. Hey, Herb is trying to take the phone away from me. I'll talk to you later, boss."

The undersheriff came on. "Hi, Bo."

"So what's up, Herb?"

"Just to let you know I haven't been sitting around here reading the paper all day. I did a little investigating."

"I told you, Herb, I don't want you doing any thinking on your own. So what did you find out?"

"As you know, Bo, anytime there's a murder you start looking for a motive. Usually, it's a family member who done it, right?"

"Right."

"For the insurance, right?"

Tully sighed. "Right"

"As you also probably know, Horace didn't have any family. His secretary, Irene Pooley, is about as close as he had to a relation or even a friend. Well, me and my insurance agent, Rob Collins, we started looking into the insurance situation. Turns out Horace had key-man insurance for two million dollars."

"What's key-man insurance?"

"I didn't know either. Rob says when there's somebody a company thinks is essential to its operation, they take out key-man insurance on him or her, to cover the loss if the person dies or something."

"And the beneficiary was?"

"The company—meaning Mike Wilson!"

"But if Wilson was murdered, too?" Tully said.

"He also had two million in key-man insurance on him, with the company as the beneficiary!"

"That's four million dollars! What happens to it if both of the insured turn up dead?"

"It goes into the company and the stockholders get it."

"You got a list of the stockholders?"

"There's only one."

"And that is?"

"Blanche Wilson."

"Wow! Okay, you done good, Herb. Maybe I'll let you do some more thinking on your own."

Herb grunted. "To tell the truth, Bo, it gave me an awful headache."

"It tends to do that. Put Lurch back on, would you, Herb?"

Lurch came on. "Yeah, boss."

"You got anything on the list of people I gave you?"

"Haven't had a chance."

"Okay. When you get to it, add the name Ben Hoot."

"Ben Hoot. You got it, boss. You want me to do this list legal or illegal?"

"Whatever it takes."

25

TULLY FOUND JANICE IN THE dining area sipping a cup of hot chocolate piled high with whipped cream. He pulled up a chair across from her. "So this is what champion lady dog-team drivers drink to keep in shape."

"They need to have some fun. Where have you been hiding, Bo?"

"Out trying to solve murders and stuff like that. And I need another favor."

"How did I ever guess."

"Look, I'm sorry I have to bother you, but dogs and a sled are about the only transportation I have available to me for this little mission."

Janice gave him an appraising look. "What's in it for me?"

Tully thought for a moment. "All the hot chocolate you can drink?"

"You know something, Bo, I should have married you when I had the chance."

"I asked you to, if you'll recall. But you had your heart set on being rich. Tom's dad was a rich banker and I was going to be a poor struggling artist. Tom is a rich banker himself now and I'm still a poor struggling artist. You made a good choice."

"Yeah," she said, smiling. "I like rich. Okay, I'll give you another ride, for old times' sake. We'd better hurry, though. It will be dark in an hour."

"The darker the better," Tully said. "Finish your hot chocolate. I want to talk to Pap and Dave before I head out again. I'll meet you up at the dog pens in an hour."

He found them in Pap's room, sitting in easy chairs, their feet propped on the coffee table. They were smoking cigars, probably Cubans. He said, "Glad to see the two of you hard at work."

"It's tough," Dave said. "Pap and I been in that hot tub so much we're turning into prunes. About time you showed up."

He told them about his visit with Ben Hoot. Pap said, "I've heard about Hoot for years. Every time somebody goes missing up on the West Branch, Hoot gets the blame."

"You think he deserves it?" Tully asked.

"No evidence ever turned up."

"I suspect not. Anyway, he gave me a lead that I'm going to follow up on. I have to tell you, this case gets weirder all the time. I talked to Lurch on the phone. He said Susan pinned Horace Baker's time of death between eleven and midnight Monday. Herb found out that both Horace and Mike had key-man insurance for two million each."

"Key-man insurance?" Pap said. "What's that?"

Tully told him. "Apparently, the way this works out is that Blanche Wilson would end up with four million dollars."

"That's a pretty fair motive," Dave said. "You don't think she killed them, do you?"

"Not personally."

"A hired killer?" Pap said. "That's always a chancy business for murder. Hit men are generally stupid. They get busted for a different murder and right away they give you up, so they can get a more lenient sentence."

Dave said, "Sounds as if you've had some experience with hit men, Pap."

"Nope. I always figured you want somebody dead you best to do it yourself."

"If you're done plotting murder," Tully said, "I'll fill you in on Mike Wilson. Lurch says that according to Susan, Wilson didn't drown—no water in his stomach or lungs. But the boot tracks from the Pout House to the river were made with Wilson's boots! How do you figure that?"

"Somebody else was wearing Wilson's boots," Dave said. "Somebody a lot lighter than Wilson. I figured that out from the tracks in the snow. The idea was to make us think Wilson had walked out to the river and drowned."

"Wilson's body was wearing the boots," Tully said.

"I don't care," Dave said.

Pap said, "The murderer must have taken the boots off Wilson and wore them down to the river to make us think Wilson had fallen in and drowned. Then he put the boots back on Wilson and threw the body in the river."

"Whoever wore the boots from the Pout House to the river had to be picked up by boat," Tully said. "So we've got at least two people involved."

Pap blew a cloud of cigar smoke at Tully. "How do you figure Mike got in the river then?"

"Whoever made the tracks to the river was too small to carry him. As Dave has pointed out, the tracks would have been much deeper if the person was carrying a body."

"They had to dump him in upstream of where we found him," Dave said. "As you pointed out, Bo, bodies don't float upstream."

Tully said, "Sometimes they do. Whoever threw him in the river wasn't aware the river was backing up. There's a back eddy by the dock and the person would have known that any body thrown in there would just float around in the eddy. I suspect the body was taken to the middle of the suspension bridge and dropped into the middle of the current."

Pap said, "Sounds reasonable. The killer probably didn't know that Mike had died before he was tossed in the river."

Dave said, "You're probably right, Bo, about him being dropped in from the suspension bridge. It's way up above the water, and the killer, or killers, probably couldn't tell the river was backing up. Normally, the body would have washed all the way down to the Blight River and from there on down to the Snake. It probably never would have been found. This way it was washed upstream."

"I guess we've solved the murder," Tully said.

"Yeah," Pap said. "Except for who did it."

"Oh, yeah, there's that," Tully said.

26

IT WAS DARK BY THE time Janice stopped the dogs outside
Cabin Three. Tully went in and came out carrying the
small kitchen table.

"What now?" Janice said.

Tully went back in and came out carrying a chair.
He sat down on the sled and asked Janice to set the
table upside-down on his lap.

"I can't believe this," she said.

"Now put the chair on the table."

She put the chair on the table. "I know," she said,
"we're going to have a private supper out here, just us
two."

"Afraid not," Tully said. "Mush us along, sweetheart. We're headed for an old snag about two hundred
yards up the groomed track."

"You've been up there before?"

"No. Why do you ask?"

"Mush!" Janice yelled. The sled took off in a spray of tails.

Minutes later, he yelled, "I think this is it!" He pointed up at a towering gray snag. He could make out the hole Ben Hoot had told him about. Janice stopped the sled and the dogs flopped down, their breaths rising like tiny clouds of fog in the moonlight.

He had Janice lift the table and chair off of him, then pushed up from the sled, grunting as he did so. It occurred to him at that moment that maybe he was getting too old to be riding dogsleds around in the dark. He set the table next to the snag, and stood the chair next to the table. He stepped on the chair and then on to the table.

"Very clever," Janice said.

"Thanks." He pulled on a white-cloth glove. "I hope a martin hasn't made its home up there." He stood on tiptoe and reached up, feeling around in the hole. His fingers touched the package. He pulled it out and looked at it.

"Find what you expected?"

"I think so," he said.

"Good. I'm getting that creepy feeling, like maybe we're being watched."

Janice walked up and pulled the lead dog around to turn the sled back down the mountain. Tully sat down on the sled and Janice loaded the table and chair back on top of him.

"I suspect we are," he said.

"Mush!"

27

THAT NIGHT TULLY LAY IN bed listening to the night sounds through an open window. The wind had come up and was blowing snow off the roof. He hoped Pap and Dave had done what he told them. This wind would cover up the tracks on the bridge even more. No doubt the West Branch Road was drifting shut, as if the avalanche weren't enough. Maybe this was the start of a blizzard. As a kid he had always looked forward to blizzards. The school superintendent would shut down all the schools, because it was too dangerous for the kids to be out. From the safety standpoint, it was the sensible thing to do. Also, it gave Tully and his friends the opportunity to spend their blizzard days out sledding. He no longer looked forward to blizzards. Something has gone wrong with a man's life, when he stops looking forward to blizzards.

The wind let up. An owl in a nearby tree let out a brief *whoo,* possibly in appreciation of some relief from the wind. Coyotes then commenced their wild laughing and giggling. Tully wondered what poor creature they had found to torment. Then a long wavering howl came down off the mountain. The coyotes instantly clammed up and were not heard from again that night. They were probably home packing their bags for a long trip out of the region. Tully wondered about the wolf. Was it part of the pack that had been decimating the elk and deer herds? For most of his life, there had been no wolves in Idaho. Then the feds, the Fish and Wildlife Service, decided to introduce them: "Wolves, here's Idaho." The wolves prospered. Tully did not like wolves, hadn't liked them since reading *Little Red Riding Hood* as a youngster. He had been pleased to see the two wolf pelts hanging in Ben Hoot's shed. He could have arrested Hoot right then on the illegal act of killing a wolf. Hoot also had known it was illegal, but both he and Tully had been too polite to mention it. Tully for one didn't relish even the possibility of getting dead over a couple of wolf pelts. In a way, he envied Hoot his lonely life. Here was a man who pretty much made up his own rules and laws and probably never violated any of them. You could probably count the number of his rules and laws on the fingers of one hand. Tully didn't want even to speculate what those rules and laws might be. Still, there was something strangely civilized about Hoot. Tully thought maybe he himself would go down to the Blight County Library when he got back and take out a couple of Willys. Well, maybe only one.

If he became too civilized, it would definitely interfere with his job.

He got up and took a sleeping pill. He didn't like sleeping pills, but sometimes one of them actually put him to sleep for a while. Waiting for the pill to work, he began to ponder his murder case. Obviously, Blanche Wilson was a central figure. She was the one who would profit from the murders of Horace Baker and Mike Wilson. It was becoming clear that she wasn't the least bit upset over the demise of her husband. Maybe Blanche was also behind the attempt to kill him and Pap with the avalanche. He knew the avalanche had been deliberately triggered with dynamite, and Blanche was the only person he had told about the approximate time he would be driving up the West Branch Road. She could have hired two hit persons, one to kill her husband this side of the avalanche and another one to kill Horace Baker on the other side, knock both of them off simultaneously. If that was the case, whoever killed Mike Wilson would still be on the lodge side, trapped there by the avalanche like everyone else. There were about forty guests to choose from. He could rule out the frat boys and Marcus Tripp, much as he hated to. He could take Lindsay off his list, too. He ruled out Janice, who already had more money and dogs than she knew what to do with. DeWayne, the bartender, was still at the top of his list, if for no other reason than he was a Scragg. That left about thirty guests, among whom was the gentleman he had flattened the evening before.

The wolf howled again. Tully didn't hear it. He had drifted off to sleep.

28

TULLY ATE BREAKFAST WITH PAP and Dave. The old man and the "Indian" had also heard the coyotes and the wolf. Dave said he liked the idea of wolves out in the wilderness, because that was what wilderness was. Pap said he liked the idea of wolves, too, but didn't care much for their reality. "They're wiping out the elk and deer."

Dave said, "How come elk and deer and wolves survived together for many thousands of years without any messing around by humankind?" Pap said it was because back then deer and elk knew how to climb trees. "Maybe there were humans too but the wolves ate them."

Tully said, "Would you two stop? We're supposed to be solving a couple of murders here." He explained his theory about two hit men, one in Blight and one trapped with them at the lodge.

Pap shook his head. "You really think Blanche is dumb enough to hire not one but two hit men? I don't think so. I told you, murder-for-hire guys give you up in the blink of an eye."

Dave said, "I don't know. Most people aren't as familiar with murder as you are, Pap. The parties involved might see it as a good deal. You give each of the killers ten grand and you pocket the rest of four million."

"These guys may be real pros," Tully said. "If one of them is up here at the lodge, he may look like any of the other guests. He probably knows how to fit in, to become part of the crowd."

"He's probably a single," Pap said. "We could get a list of the guests and pick out the single guys. If I was going to murder someone, I certainly wouldn't want my wife along, particularly my wife, no offense to your mother, Bo."

"None taken."

"I'll talk to Blanche and have her get me a list. It should be easy enough to pick out the singles."

Dave said, "Yeah, but if the hit man was a real pro, wouldn't he bring a woman along just as part of his cover? She wouldn't even have to know what he was up to."

Tully said, "Stop complicating things, Dave. I want to get out of this place sometime soon."

After breakfast Tully stopped by the lodge office. Blanche was nowhere to be seen, but Lois was seated at a desk working on a stack of papers. She told Tully she didn't think there would be a problem with the list of guests, but she would have to ask Blanche first. "Jobs aren't all that easy to find in these parts," she said. "By the way, aren't you supposed to have a warrant when you go after things like private lists?"

"A what?" Tully said.

Lois laughed. "I forgot, it's the Blight way. Okay, I'll get you the list, one way or another."

"I'd appreciate it. Say, I need to use your phone, Lois."

"Help yourself, Sheriff."

"My point is, I need you out of the office, with the door closed."

"Oh," she said. "I'll go get myself a cup of coffee."

"Good idea. Get me one too, if you don't mind."

"You got it, Sheriff." She left.

Tully called the National Guard headquarters and asked the pilot to pick up a package. "I'll be there in an hour," Ron Stolz said.

Then he called his own office. Daisy answered.

"Good news, Bo!" she said. "The highway department says they'll have the West Branch Road cleared by Sunday."

"Daisy, good news would be if they had it cleared right now. I'm even starting to miss you."

"Really, Bo?"

"Yeah, really. Now put Lurch on, will you?"

"Byron!" she yelled in his ear. "Bo wants you on line one."

Lurch picked up. "Hi, boss."

"I'm sending you a package by helicopter, Lurch.

Get out to the National Guard base and pick it up. Should be there in about two hours."

"What's in the package?"

"I was getting to that. Actually, the package is now in a shoe box I found. The object in the shoe box is in a Ziploc bag like they put leftovers and stuff in. Be careful when you take the bag out of the shoe box because I want you to check it for prints."

"Okay. So what's the object in the bag?"

"I was getting to that, too. It's a gun in a holster. Check both the gun and the holster for prints and if you find some, see if you can get a match on the bullet that killed Baker. Check the clip and cartridges for prints, too."

"Got it, boss. What kind of gun?"

"Lurch, would you let me tell this! I'm pretty sure it's a Colt Woodsman."

"That's a .22 caliber. The cartridges are pretty small but I might get a partial print off one of them. You think it could be the gun used on Horace Baker?"

"Could be but I don't see how."

"If it's the gun used on Baker, why wouldn't the killer deep-six it?"

"If the killer happens to be a gun lover, and the gun happens to be an original Colt Woodsman, as I think it is, he probably couldn't bear to deep-six it. I actually don't think it was used on Baker, because how would it get back here?"

"Geez, boss, I don't know. Why ask me?"

"It was a rhetorical question, Lurch. I'll call you about five, to see what you find out."

"Daisy wants to talk to you."

Daisy came on. "More good news, Bo. One of the deputies caught Clarence!"

"Caught him! He was supposed to shoot him! Where's Clarence now?"

"We have him in a cell. Stubb Speizer is furious, because I had him moved into a cell with Lister Scragg. We couldn't leave them in the same cell, because Stubb would get bitten."

Tully ran his fingers back through his hair. "Did you think about calling the pound?"

"The pound would put him down, you know that, Bo. He's such a cute little dog."

"Daisy, one way or another, you make sure Clarence is off the premises by the time I get back. By 'premises,' I mean the earth!"

"But he is so cute, boss."

Cute, thought Tully. Cute is what keeps most of the pets in the country alive. If they all looked like maggots they would be fish bait.

29

TULLY TRAMPED OUT THROUGH THE snow to the helicopter.
He handed the shoe box to a National Guard airman
and waved at Ron Stolz, the pilot. Ron waved back and
then lifted off.

Tully crossed the road and walked down to the
dock on the river. Whoever made the tracks from the
Pout House to the river had to be picked up by boat.
As far as he knew, the inflatable jet boat was the only
boat anywhere on the river. But Grady would probably
know if the inflatable had been moved. It would be a
simple matter to launch another jet boat somewhere else
on the river. In any case, at least two persons had to be
involved in the death of Mike Wilson: the person who
made the tracks and the person who drove the boat to
pick up the first person. Tully had somehow managed
the jet outboard well enough to survive several horrific

sets of rapids. He had no intention of doing it again in his entire life and could scarcely believe that he and Lurch had made it back alive. Whoever drove a boat up here must have been incredibly skilled or incredibly stupid.

He climbed up to the suspension bridge, which was covered with packed snow. It appeared that several dozen people had walked back and forth across the bridge in the last day, wiping out any previous set of tracks. The middle of the bridge was a good thirty feet above the water, with the strongest part of the current passing directly below. If the river had started to back up this far by the time the body was dropped in, it was doubtful the person doing the dropping would have been aware of it. He headed back across the bridge.

He stopped by the office on his way into the lodge. Lois said she had checked with Blanche. Tully could have the list. "I ran off a copy for you." She handed it to him.

"Wow, that's service," he said. He thanked her and headed through the lounge to the dining room. Lindsay was seated on one of the sofas, her crutches beside her. "Bo, it's about time you showed up. I've been waiting for you ever since the helicopter took off. I thought maybe you hopped aboard it."

"I was tempted. So, does my secret investigator have any more interesting info for me?"

"No, I stayed up until two o'clock watching Mrs. Wilson's apartment, but nobody came out. This detective work is getting to be a real drag."

"Tell me about it! Anyway, I have a new job for a

smart math major like yourself." He folded the guest list and gave it to her. "Don't tell anybody about this or that you're working for me. We could have some fairly dangerous people running around here. What I want you to do is go through this list and pick out all the single guests and see if there seems to be anything unusual about them. Then I want you to match the name up with the individual. Tonight at dinner you can point out any suspects for me, surreptitiously, of course."

"What kind of person exactly am I looking for?"

"Either a hit man or a hit woman."

"Oh great!"

"Listen, Lindsay, you don't have to do it if it scares you."

"No, it'll be fun. Maybe when I get back to school, I'll change my major from math to law enforcement."

"Take my advice, stick with math."

Tulley found Janice seated by herself in the dining room. "Mind if I join you."

"My pleasure, Bo."

He pulled out a chair and sat down. "You been out working the dogs?"

"Yeah, I drove them up to Cabin Three, but I don't think I'll go back there again."

"Why? You see something?"

"No, it's just that I get this eerie feeling. Maybe it's because I saw the way you reacted that time, jerking out your gun."

"Probably a good idea to stay clear of that place, all right."

"Yeah, I think so. By the way. Tom seems to be missing."

"What makes you think so?"

"I've been trying to call him ever since they got the phone line hooked up and he's never home."

"Probably out having a beer. No reason to stay home, if you're not there."

"I wouldn't want something to happen to him. He could be in the hospital or lying on the floor at home unconscious."

"Or having an affair," Tully said.

"Or having an affair," she said, smiling slightly.

"I can tell you this, sweetheart, men get over an affair a lot faster than they do a stroke or a heart attack. So just hope it isn't anything more serious than an affair."

"You're such a thoughtful person, Bo."

"I try to be."

The waitress came for their orders. Janice took the hot turkey sandwich with gravy and mashed potatoes. Tully went with the clam strips and french fries.

30

AFTER LUNCH, TULLY WENT UPSTAIRS and knocked on the door of the Wilson apartment. Blanche opened the door. "Oh, hi, Bo."

"I haven't seen you in a while, Blanche. You been hiding out?"

"I guess I have. I haven't felt like talking to people. Everything is such a mess. Mike and I haven't got along for years, and I didn't think his murder would affect me so much. And then for Horace to be killed, too. Please come in, Bo."

Tully followed her into her Danish Modern living room. Tully had once liked Danish Modern, but no longer. He had seen too much of it and guessed it must now practically drive the Danes themselves mad. Blanche indicated for him to sit on a couch. She sat down in a facing easy chair.

"Would you like anything to drink, Bo?"

"No thanks, I just had lunch. I really hate to disturb you, Blanche, but I have some questions I need answered."

"Fire away," she said, folding her hands in her lap.

"Did you know that Horace and Mike had each taken out key-man insurance on the other."

"No. I've never even heard of key-man insurance."

"It's a policy that companies sometimes take out on persons they feel are essential to their operation. The idea is that the insurance covers some of the loss if an important person somehow expires or is otherwise disabled."

"I see," she said. "In this case, both Mike and Horace were caused to expire. So who is the beneficiary?"

"The company. And you now seem to be the company, Blanche."

"Good heavens! How much money are we talking about, Bo?"

"Four million dollars."

Blanche sucked in her breath. She sat in silence for several seconds, staring at him in disbelief. Then she said, "That would be a motive for murder."

"Yes, it would."

"I don't know what to say. Probably I shouldn't say anything. Obviously, I didn't murder Mike and Horace. But you're thinking maybe I had it done, aren't you, Bo?"

"The thought crossed my mind. Four million dollars is a lot of money. But I'm really not accusing you of anything, Blanche. I simply want you to know that anyone looking at this case would realize you had a motive, the most common motive in the world."

"I'm aware of that. But I didn't do it. I would never even think of doing such a thing. And if I did think of it, I wouldn't know how to pull it off."

"I don't know how it was pulled off, but I do know that both Mike and Horace were murdered. And I need your cooperation to get to the bottom of this thing."

Blanche pulled a handkerchief out of the sleeve of her blouse and dabbed at her eyes. "I don't know anything," she said, her voice cracking.

"Would it be all right if I looked through Mike's gun cabinets?"

"Bo, you can do anything you think might solve these murders. Wait till I get the key." She went into the kitchen and returned. "Follow me. I'll show you where his den is. He called it his den, but actually it's his bedroom. We've had separate bedrooms for a year or more."

"I take it he wasn't a particularly nice man."

"No, he wasn't. If I had killed him, Bo, it wouldn't have been for money."

She showed him two huge cabinets with glass doors. She unlocked both of them and then left the room. The first cabinet was devoted to rifles and shotguns, the other to handguns. The handgun cabinet contained thirty or so semiautomatics and revolvers, each hanging by its trigger guard from a wooden peg. Despite his years in law enforcement, or perhaps because of it, Tully had no great love of guns. He had deputies who could recite the entire history of almost any firearm ever manufactured. He chose to rely on their knowledge rather than pursue the subject himself. His primary concern was that his own gun fire when he needed it to. He noticed there was one empty peg. That interested him more than the guns. Most of the gun nuts he knew would never think of selling any part of their collections. Individual guns were too much a part of their personal identity. So the empty peg was a matter of particular interest. If there had once been a gun on the peg, why would Mike Wilson want to get rid of it? Of equal interest, the three pegs next in the same row contained Colt Woodsmans, no doubt originals.

He found Blanche seated on a stool in the kitchen. Her hands were clenched together and she appeared to be shaking. Even though Blanche Wilson was at the moment his prime suspect, he felt sorry for her. Tully often felt sorry for murderers.

"Thanks," he said to her.

She nodded mutely.

He let himself out.

31

HE FOUND PAP AND DAVE in the recreation room, which was equipped with about every piece of exercise equipment known to man. They were shooting pool.

"I see you two are busy working out."

"Yeah," Dave said. "It's exhausting, too."

Pap said, "The reason Dave is sweating, I've already taken him for twenty bucks."

Tully said, "I would have thought an old tracker like you, Dave, could spot a pool hustler at a hundred yards."

He told them about inspecting the suspension bridge. "I'm pretty sure Mike's body was dropped off the middle of the suspension bridge. I'm not sure that tells us much, though."

Pap said, "I don't know about that. It tells us that at least one of the persons involved probably was familiar with the back eddy by the dock. So he had been down to the dock in daylight and realized the body would have to be dropped in from the middle of the bridge, if he wanted to get it into the main current."

"So you think the killer, or one of the killers, might be a regular at the lodge, or even one of the employees," Tully said.

"Seems reasonable."

Dave said, "You want me to take a look at the tracks, Bo?"

"Sure. People have been out tramping back and forth over it, so I don't know if the tracks will mean anything. But see what you can find. Take Pap with you. He's generally useless but maybe he can turn up something. He's had a lot of experience with dead bodies."

"Thanks," Pap said.

Dave said, "Maybe you can get Lurch back up here to take some impressions."

"I don't think it would help."

"Maybe the impressions would match Mike Wilson's boots," Pap said.

"Are you trying to drive me crazy?"

Dave chalked his cue, then knocked the six-ball into a corner pocket. Next he drove the eight-ball into the same pocket with a three-cushion shot.

Tully whistled appreciatively. "Just goes to show a wasted childhood has some worth after all."

"Thanks," Dave said.

"Get out of here, Bo," Pap said. "You're costing me money."

At five o'clock, Tully went into the lodge office. It

was empty. He phoned the department. "What have you got for me, Lurch?"

"I don't think you're going to be happy with this, Boss," the CSI unit said.

"Try me."

"Just as you suspected, the gun is an original Colt Woodsman. The striations on the bullet that killed Baker match the one from the test shot. Whoever used it probably couldn't stand to deep-six it. Probably figured he would wait until the ruckus over the murder died down and then go back and collect it."

"That's what I thought. In one of his gun cabinets, Mike Wilson had three original Colt Woodsmans on pegs in a row and one empty peg at the end of the row. He obviously was collecting Woodsmans."

"Looks that way."

"How about prints?"

"Sorry to tell you this, boss, but no prints on either the package or the gun. They'd been wiped clean."

"Not even on the clip or cartridges?"

"Nope. Somebody went to the trouble of wiping away every possible print."

Tully slumped into Lois's chair. "What does this mean, Lurch?"

"It means we can't tie the gun to Wilson with prints."

"If he was collecting Woodsmans, he probably has the serial number on the gun registered somewhere, at least with his insurance company."

"And if you can show the gun is part of Wilson's collection, what?"

"It means that whoever shot Horace Baker had to have access to Wilson's gun cabinet. And the gun cabinet is locked. So he, or she, had to know where the key was."

"Like Mrs. Wilson?"

"Like Mrs. Wilson. But the gun had to be taken out before the avalanche. Don't ask me how it got back on this side of the avalanche."

"I was about to ask you that."

"I knew you were. Is Herb around?"

"I'll get him for you."

"Hey, Herb!" Lurch shouted in Tully's ear. "Boss wants you on line one!"

We definitely have to do some work on phone protocol, Tully thought.

"Hi, Bo," Herb said. "How did you know I was resting?"

"A lucky guess. I want you to check the last couple weeks of phone records from the lodge into Blight City. Look for anything that might seem unusual. If several calls go to a particular residence, find out who lives there. Maybe you'll find a pattern of some kind."

"If you're looking for a hit man, I doubt you'll find him in Blight."

"In this instance, Herb, I'm not looking for a hit man, but if you turn one up, that's okay, too."

32

TULLY FOUND THE HANDYMAN IN his shop working on a piece of equipment.

"I hate to bother you, Grady, but I need another lift up the mountain."

"Yes sir, Sheriff. Hold on just one minute. I need to tighten a belt on this snowblower. One of these days I'm going to have to blow a lot of snow. Blanche has been so upset lately, she hasn't bothered me about it, but I'm afraid the time is coming."

"How well do you know her?"

"Pretty well. I've worked for the Wilsons pretty close to five years now, and she's always been fair to me. I get my little house to live in and a decent salary. Along with my retirement from the air force, I manage fine."

Grady made a couple of turns with his crescent wrench. "Mostly, I stay up here at the lodge. Sometimes

I drive down to Blight City, but then where am I? Blight City! So I turn around and come back. There, that does it for the snowblower."

The Sno-Cat pulled to a stop next to the Cabin Three trail. Tully tossed out a pair of snowshoes.

"Wait for me, Grady. I should be back in an hour or so. If I'm not, you might as well go home."

"If you're going in to see old Hoot again, I don't recommend it."

"It's not my favorite outing," Tully said, fastening the harnesses on the snowshoes. "Particularly since the last time he told me not to come back again."

Grady nodded his head. "Pretty good advice."

Even before Tully sighted the old woodsman's cabin, he sensed his presence. He turned and looked at a thick cluster of trees. "Come on out, Hoot, I know you're there."

Hoot stepped out from behind the trees. He had the hammer back on his rifle. This time he was fully dressed. "That's a problem with making another bad shot on a skunk, Bo. Makes it difficult to stay hid. I thought I told you I didn't want to see you back up here."

"That's a problem with being sheriff, Hoot. There's a whole passel of folks don't want me back again. But I've got a job to do. If you want to be rid of me for good, you better help me with this murder."

"I don't care one way or the other about your murder. I didn't do it. If I'd done it, there wouldn't be all this fuss."

"I know you didn't do it. The folks who did do it

thought they would be clever. As you probably know, the dumbest way to murder a person is to try and be clever."

"That would be my opinion."

To Tully's relief, the old man lowered the hammer on his rifle. "You told me I could find what I was looking for in the hollow tree. I found it, exactly what I was looking for. The problem is, the item had all the fingerprints wiped off."

"Sounds like a good idea."

"Without the fingerprints, Hoot, the object isn't much good to me. That was a moonlit night, when the fellow hid the object there. I figure it was bright enough for you to recognize the person."

"You figure that, do you?" Hoot snapped back the hammer on his rifle.

"Yes, I do. And I want to know right now who it was."

"If I told you who it was, then the next thing you would want is for me to testify to that fact in court."

"You got that exactly right."

Hoot shook his head. "You're the craziest fellow I've ever seen. People think I'm crazy, but I couldn't hold a candle to you, Bo, when it comes to crazy."

"Thanks," Tully said. "Actually I'm not sure you would have to testify, Hoot. But there's a possibility it might work out that way. I figure you better know it now."

"I guess I can either shoot you or tell you."

"That about covers it. So tell me."

"Mike Wilson."

33

"MIKE WILSON!" PAP SAID. THEY were seated in the dining room.

"Not so loud," Tully hissed at him.

He had told Pap and Dave about his visit to Ben Hoot.

"You're lucky he didn't shoot you," Dave said.

"He might still shoot you, he gets a chance," Pap said.

"Why do you think I'm telling you two? In any case, don't mention Hoot's connection with this. If I haul him into court to testify, he probably will shoot me."

"The trick is to figure out how the gun got back to Mike Wilson," Dave said. "Obviously, Mike must have been behind the killing of Horace Baker."

"I figure he had to be, but I don't know how."

Someone put a hand on Tully's shoulder. He jumped.

"You've got to calm down, Bo," Lindsay said.

"And you've got to stop doing that, Lindsay. Next time I'll probably shoot you. Sit down. We'll get you something to eat."

"I've already had dinner," she said. "With him." She pointed across the room. Marcus Tripp was sitting at a table by himself.

"I can't believe you ate dinner with Marcus," Tully said. "I realize you have pretty thin pickings in the man crop these days, but I have to tell you, Marcus is a weaky. You don't want to get tangled up with a weaky."

"It's no big deal," she said. "But I got to thinking about what you said, how hard it is to find a good man nowadays. So I decided I better hold on to Marcus until something better comes along. Also, his father is rich."

"Rich is not to be sneezed at," Dave said.

"It's a factor," Lindsay said. "He's also kind of romantic."

"He may have several good qualities, too," Tully said. "So how are you doing on my list?"

"Okay. It's harder than I thought. Should have something for you tomorrow. Is it all right if I mention the other thing now?" She nodded at Dave and Pap.

"They're highly unreliable," Tully said. "But tell me anyway."

"The man was back last night. Left Mrs. Wilson's apartment at exactly two-fourteen a.m. I had almost given up and headed for bed."

Pap said, "Bo has you on a stakeout?"

"Yeah," she said. "You see the circles under my eyes?"

"Please tell me you recognized him," Tully said.

"No, I didn't. It's dark at that end of the hall. I didn't want to follow him. Who knows, he could be the murderer!"

"There you go, thinking of yourself again," Tully said. "You're just like all my other deputies."

"But it's something, isn't it, Bo?"

"I'm kidding you, Lindsay. It is in fact a lot. We'll figure out who this chap is sooner or later. And you're right, he could be our murderer. But tonight I want you in bed no later than nine. You do have black circles under your eyes."

"I'll come tuck you in, sweetheart," Pap said.

"You will not," Tully said. "She will tuck herself in."

"But Pap is my buddy," Lindsay said.

Tully rolled his eyes heavenward. Pap grinned.

Dave said, "Pap and I checked out the footbridge like you asked, Bo. There are so many tracks going back and forth, it's almost impossible to find a sign worth anything. There was one small area protected from the wind by a post and we could make out a section where the snow had been flattened by something. Right next to it was another flattened area, maybe two inches deeper. That mean anything to you?"

"No."

"Good," Pap said. "It didn't mean nothing to us either."

34

TULLY FOUND THE FOUR WSU frat boys playing cards in the lounge. He stopped at their table. They looked up at him belligerently.

"I understand you guys beat up one of my men?"

The belligerent looks faded. "You mean the Indian?" one of the boys said.

"I didn't have anything to do with it."

"Me neither," said another one, shaking his head. "It was Lance."

The largest of the four, the bruises still showing on his face, said, "I didn't beat him up, he beat me up. I never knew Indians were so fast. He's lucky he didn't kill me."

"You're the lucky one," Tully said. "Dave doesn't have an off switch if he gets mad. So you're lucky he didn't get mad. Even so, he starts something, he finishes it. I guess he was only playing with you. He's not really an Indian anyway. He pretends to be, so he can get his own casino. Now the only reason I'm bothering even to talk to you four thumb-suckers is Mrs. Wilson told me you like to think you're into extreme sports."

Lance said, "We were going to climb the back side of Mount Blight, but the avalanche threat up there got too high. Just because we're not stupid doesn't mean we don't like extreme sports."

"You're not stupid? I was hoping you were, because I have something I want you to do. The lodge owner has asked me to think up an exercise for you, something to keep you out of her hair. And her bar."

"Like what?" Lance said.

"Follow me." Tully led them over to the 3-D map. "I assume you're all fair skiers."

Lance, who seemed to be the leader of the group, said, "We're great skiers!"

"Excellent," Tully said. "I need four guys with an exaggerated opinion of themselves. Now, pay attention." He pointed at the map and explained the exercise he had thought up.

"Piece of cake," Lance said.

"Finally you ski back to the lodge. You should complete the exercise in less than six hours."

"How do we do that?"

"I'm glad you asked that, Lance, because now I'm going to tell you."

He told them.

"Anyone ever do that before?" a kid asked.

"Don't pay any attention to Rodney," Lance said. "What's in it for us, Sheriff?"

"I thought you might ask that, Lance. A hundred dollars each, if you're back within six hours. Nothing if you're late. In any case, it will give Mrs. Wilson a day without your company."

"A hundred bucks is chicken feed," the one called Wiggy said. He was thin and wore glasses and appeared somewhat more intelligent than the others.

"I thought it might be," Tully said. "But that's as high as I go."

"Sounds like a lot of work for not much," the kid known as Turk said. What appeared to be a diamond stickpin pierced one of his eyebrows. Tully imagined the adornment pleased the kid's rich father enormously. "I'd rather sit around here all day and drink," Turk added.

"That's part of the problem," Tully said. "Tell you what? You guys do this for me, and I'll let you participate in a murder trial. How does that sound?"

"Hey, cool!" the four said almost in unison.

"Now it is possible the exercise can't be done in six hours," Tully said. "Maybe one of you falls and breaks a leg or something. In that case, I don't want any of you to leave him. I assume you all have cell phones."

"Yeah," Lance said.

"So in case of an accident, you call the Sheriff's Department at 911, and I'll have it arranged so a helicopter picks you up."

"If the guy is dead, it's okay to leave him, isn't it?" Lance said.

"Well, yeah," Tully said. "If you're sure he's dead."

35

AT EIGHT-THIRTY THE NEXT MORNING, Tully and Grady towed the four frat boys on their skis up to the top of the ridge with a rope tied to the back of the Sno-Cat. The four were in rowdy good spirits.

"You're probably wondering, Grady, what I have planned for these young men. Basically, I want them out of the lodge for a day. They have become an enormous irritation to Blanche. And, more important, to me."

"Yes sir," Grady said. "To me also. There's some pretty rugged terrain up here. They could get themselves killed if they're not careful."

"Yeah, but there's always a downside. Keep in mind that we send young men like these off to war all the time to get them wounded and killed and their heads messed up. That's what we old men do to young men, don't you know that? It's our revenge for them being young."

"Yes sir."

"We do it mostly to poor young men."

"Yes sir."

"These are rich young men, of course. On the other hand, this isn't a war."

"Yes sir."

When they arrived at the top of the ridge, Tully had Grady drive down to where the Sno-Cat had turned around previously. The frat boys skied up to Tully. He checked his watch. "It's almost nine. You have to be back at the lodge before three.

"I'm in charge, right, Sheriff?" Lance said.

"You're in charge, Lance. If you get hurt or killed, then Rodney takes over."

A cheer went up from the other two.

"That sort of thing happens to me all the time," Tully said. "Too bad you don't have someone to watch your back, Lance."

Tully checked his watch as the quartet of skiers swept down the slope past the snowy sculptures of buried trees. "Three o'clock!" he yelled after them. "Don't be late!"

"You think it can be done?" Grady asked him.

"I don't know. The main thing is it keeps them out of my sight for a day."

"You have something against fraternity boys, Sheriff?"

"Yes, I do, Grady. I was an independent in college. The frat boys were the ones who got all the good-looking girls in the sororities."

"I never went to college," Grady said.

"You didn't miss much," Tully said. "If you were a frat boy, it was fun. You majored in PE or pre-law or something else that didn't require a whole lot of study that might interfere with your fun. If you were an independent, you had to major in something where you could get a job after you graduated. So you had to take something hard. If it was fun or easy, like psychology, everyone would major in it and you would have all that competition for a job after graduation. Something hard could be pure torture."

"What did you major in?"

"Art."

"That sounds like a lot of fun to me, Sheriff."

"It was. Why do you think I ended up as a hick cop for a hick county?"

"Yes sir, I did wonder about that."

"You can stop wondering."

"Yes sir."

36

WHEN HE GOT BACK TO the lodge, Lois was seated at her desk in the office.

"Mind if I borrow your phone a minute, Lois?"

"What if I said yes?"

"I would use it anyway."

"That's what I thought. I really don't mind, Bo. Use it all you want. Would you like me to step out of the office?"

"Not this time, Lois. Just don't go blabbing anything you might hear."

"I'll do my best."

Tully dialed. Daisy answered. "Boss, if you're not back here soon, I think I'll quit!"

"You can't quit, Daisy. You have to give thirty days notice, and I'll be back by then. What's the problem anyway?"

"Nobody knows what to do! I try to tell them, but of course they won't listen to me."

"Herb is supposed to be in charge."

"Oh, you know they don't listen to Herb either. Besides, he's gone most of the time checking on some stuff you gave him."

The general state of confusion in the office actually made him feel better. Maybe he was important to the operation after all. That would certainly be a motive for anyone trying to kill him. Maybe the person who set off the avalanche knew what he was doing. With Tully gone, the murders would no doubt go unsolved. Killing Pap as a bonus was probably a good idea, too, because otherwise someone would die for the murder of Bo Tully. It might not be the right person, but somebody would die. Pap was a sentimental kind of guy.

"Listen, Daisy, is Herb around there now?"

"He just came in, boss. I hope you chew on him good!"

Tully covered the earpiece while Daisy yelled at Herb to take line one.

"Hi, Bo," Herb said. "Hope you're not paying any attention to Daisy. She's been flipping out ever since you've been gone. You don't have something going with her, do you?"

"Not yet, Herb. She's in the middle of a divorce."

"Well, I imagine Albert the Awful won't be too upset to be rid of her."

"So what do you have for me, Herb?"

"Nothing much, Bo, except I've been running a real tight ship while you've been gone."

"That's great, Herb."

"Do I get a raise?"

"No. I assume you have disposed of Clarence."

"I'm working myself up for it."

"You don't have to work yourself up for it. Just do it."

"Right, Bo."

"Now get me back to Daisy."

Daisy picked up. "What now, boss?"

"I just wanted to make sure Brian Pugh is out taking care of the little task I assigned him."

"It's taken care of. Lurch told me and I told Brian. He's out there right now handling it. I made sure of that."

"Good."

Daisy loved ordering people around.

Tully hung up. "I forgot you were sitting there, Lois. Don't tell anyone what you heard."

"All I could make out of interest, Sheriff, was that you might be dating some woman called Daisy who is getting a divorce."

"That's the part I don't want you to tell anyone."

Lois said, "I hope you don't think Blanche had anything to do with the murder of Mike Wilson."

"What I think doesn't amount to anything, Lois. It's only what I can prove. And right now I can't prove a thing."

37

TULLY FOUND THE HANDYMAN IN his shop. "You ever know Mike Wilson to buy dynamite, Grady?"

Grady thought for a moment. "He was going to blast a new channel for that crick that meanders through the meadow down the road. I never knew anybody that wanted to straighten a crick before, but that's the kind of person Mike was. He liked everything nice and tidy, even cricks. You'll notice in the shop, there's a place marked out on the pegboard for every tool. If he found a tool that hadn't been put back in its proper place, he'd blow a fuse."

"Did he ever straighten the creek?"

"No, sir, he never did."

"What happened to the dynamite?"

"Can't rightly say. Never heard Mike mention it or the crick again."

"When did he purchase the dynamite?"

"How come you're so interested in dynamite, Sheriff? Somebody blow something up?"

"Maybe. So when did Mike buy it?"

"Last summer sometime, when he got all fussed up over the crick wasting so much of the meadow. To tell you the truth, I like the crick the way it is."

"Me too," Tully said. "You're sure he purchased the dynamite?"

"Pretty sure. He said he did. Said it made him nervous, driving it back up to the lodge in the back of his car. Apparently it is the kind of dynamite that a sudden jolt can set it off, like if another car rams you from behind."

Tully said, "Back when I was a kid, it was called ditching dynamite. Don't know what they call it now. It doesn't seem to me to be the sort of thing you want to have lying around."

"You're making me nervous, Sheriff."

"Hope so, Grady. You might take a look around the shop, see if you can turn up any."

"Yes sir!"

Tully met Pap and Dave for lunch. "Looks as if this might be our last free meal," he told them. "You better order the most expensive dish they've got."

"Glad you told us," Pap said.

The waitress came to take their orders. Pap and Dave each ordered the T-bone steak.

"Oh," the waitress said, "those are served only for dinner in the evening."

"This is an emergency," Tully told her. "My men need T-bone steaks right now. Otherwise, I can't be responsible for what they might do."

The waitress smiled. "Okay, Sheriff. I have orders to give you anything you ask for.

"Anything?"

"In the way of food," she said, laughing. "But I would be happy to discuss any other matters you might have in mind."

"That's a discussion I'll look forward to," he told her. "Otherwise, today has been nothing but one disappointment after another. I'll take the soup and salad combo."

The waitress left, smiling. Not bad, Tully thought.

"Soup and salad," Dave said. "Bo, that doesn't give you anywhere near your daily requirement of cholesterol."

"I know," he said. "But I've got at least ten pounds I have to drop. Then I'll stop by your House of Fry and order one of your chicken-fried steaks."

"Gain all ten pounds back in one meal," Dave said.

"That's my plan. Anyway, here's what I have up till now. I know the avalanche was deliberately set off by ditching dynamite. The marks are still up in the snow on the ridge where the avalanche started. From that point, you can clearly see the road down below, and it would be easy to see the red Explorer coming up the road. I just found out from Grady that Mike bought some ditching dynamite last summer. He had to have a permit from Alcohol, Tobacco, Firearms and Explosives to do that, and he had to fill out a form to get the permit. When we get back to town, we'll get a copy from ATF."

"You have any evidence of the dynamite, Bo?"

"Just the marks in the snow and the holes. I think Mike buried the dynamite at the top of an old rockslide. I'll hunt somebody down with a digital camera and see if I can get some pictures."

After lunch, Tully found Lindsay in the lounge playing chess with Marcus. The boy gave Tully a sheepish look.

"You should be out of here tomorrow, Marcus," Tully said. "Then you'll have the chance to explain to your daddy how you drowned your BMW."

"I already explained it to him over the phone. I thought it would be safer that way. And I would just as soon you didn't talk to him, Sheriff, because I may have modified the facts a little."

"That's certainly what I would have done, Marcus. I think you may have the makings of a fine lawyer. Now I need to borrow your partner here for a private consultation."

He led Lindsay into the 3-D map room.

"What's up, Bo?"

"Tell me you have a digital camera with you."

"Sure, you want to borrow it?"

"No, I'm not much of a tech freak. I need you to shoot some pictures for me."

"Great!"

"And then you'll probably get to testify as a witness in a trial."

"Cool!"

"Yes, it is. I'll pick you up out in front of the lodge in an hour. Come bundled up."

"Where are you going now?"

"I have to arrange transportation."

Janice was still eating lunch. "A passenger!" she exclaimed.

"Yeah," Tully said. "But she doesn't weigh much. The extra weight may slow the mutts down a bit, but that's all."

"Calling them mutts isn't helping you one bit to get that ride. Who is the passenger?"

"Lindsay Blair."

"That hot little fox!"

"Hey, there's nothing between us. She's just a kid."

"When did that ever stop you? I was a kid once, too, you may remember."

"And then you married Tom. By the way, did he ever turn up?"

"Yeah, his aunt Margaret died and he drove up to Lewiston for the funeral."

"See, just what I told you. And you thought he was having an affair!"

"Men lie."

"Oh, sure, there's that. Anyway, are you going to haul me and my passenger up the ridge again? I could ask Grady, but I'd just as soon he doesn't know what I'm up to."

"Is he a suspect?"

"Everybody is a suspect."

"Am I a suspect."

"Sure. But not of murder."

Janice smiled. "Good."

38

"COOL!" LINDSAY SAID WHEN SHE saw the sled and dogs.

"I thought you might like it," Tully said.

He sat down on the sled and tucked Lindsay's crutches in on each side of him. She wiggled in between his knees and wrapped her arms around his legs.

"This kid knows all the moves," Janice muttered. "Mush!"

The pups took off full speed up the slope, scarcely noticing the extra weight, as far as Tully could tell. They arrived at the site of the avalanche in the same mad scramble as before, the dogs ready for a complete tour of the mountain.

"You need to work them more," Tully told Janice.

"Already you're an expert on sled dogs."

"Yes, well, in my judgment you will have no trouble winning the race with this team. I wish my detectives had half their enthusiasm." He slipped his hands under Lindsay's bottom and pushed her up. He handed her the crutches. Then he pushed himself up, grunting slightly as he did so. The grunting did not go unnoticed by Janice.

"Maybe you need to work out a bit more at the gym," she told him.

"I hate exercise in all its meaningless forms," he replied. He walked down to one of the gray holes, squatted, and pointed. "Can you get a shot of this, Lindsay?"

"Yes. Do you want yourself in the shot?"

"Of course. I need to be in it to show the proportions."

"You could have brought a yardstick," Janice said. "That would have shown the proportions even better."

"Yardsticks don't have to win elections. How does my hair look?"

"Lovely," Janice said.

"What are those splotches, anyway?" Lindsay asked.

"The remains of dynamite blasts," Tully said. "You may have to testify you took the picture."

"Do I get to testify, too?" Janice said.

"That can be arranged. You are a witness."

Lindsay said, "I've taken four shots. How many do you want, Bo?"

"Depends," Tully said, climbing back up to her. "Let me have a look at them."

Lindsey brought up each of the photos on the LCD monitor and showed him. "Good," he said. "I'm even handsomer than I thought."

"Which is saying quite a bit," Janice said.

"I don't think Janice likes you very much, Bo," Lindsay said.

"She loves me, Lindsay. All women do."

Janice laughed. "He could be right about that, kid."

Tully said, "One more favor, Janice. Run us over again to Cabin Three."

"I hate that place," she said. "It gives me the creeps."

"It gives me the creeps, too, but I need to check something out."

Marge Honeycut's snowmobile was parked outside of Cabin Three. Lindsay and Janice sat on the sled while Tully went into the cabin.

Tully said, "Marge, what are you doing in a crime scene?"

"What crime scene?"

"The crime scene I should have put a crime-scene tape around so you would know it was a crime scene."

"The only crime I noticed here, Bo, is the rotten little squirrels got in again and chewed up something all over the floor."

"I take it you swept the mess up."

"Sure."

"Where is it?"

"I dumped it in this plastic bag." She showed him the bag.

"The bag have anything else in it before you dumped in the mess?"

"Nope, it was empty."

"Good, let me look in the bag."

Marge held the bag open for him. He looked in. "Excellent! You done good, Marge." He took the bag from her and tied a knot in it. He took a felt pen from his pocket. "Watch what I'm doing, Marge." He wrote the date and time on the bag and then drew a mark across the knot.

"I seen what you done. You wrote the date and time on it. What's the mark on the knot for?"

"To keep people from messing with it. Do you know what this means?"

"No."

"It means, Marge, you may have to testify in a murder trial."

She clapped her hands together. "Wonderful!" She went out, started her snowmobile, and rode off.

Janice yelled at him. "Hurry up, Bo. I'm getting that creepy feeling."

"Lindsay!" Tully yelled out the door. "Bring your camera in here."

She came in a rush, her crutches flailing through the snow. "What, Bo?"

"I'm going to crouch down over here and point at this little dark spot on the floor. Can you get a picture of it and me."

"Sure, there's a flash on the camera."

She snapped the photo.

"Take a couple more at different angles," he told her.

She took several more pictures.

"How's my hair?" he said.

"Still good."

"Can I have the memory card?"

She took it out and gave it to him. "There may be some pictures of me on it," she said.

"No problem."

"Naked."

"No problem."

He heard something rustle behind him and spun around, his hand reaching inside his jacket. A squirrel was sitting on a kitchen shelf staring at him. It had a pine cone in its mouth.

"You almost gave me a heart attack, squirrel, but I planned on taking you with me."

"It's only a cute little squirrel," Lindsay said. "You have to calm down, Bo. You're getting way too jumpy."

Cute gets on my nerves, he thought. "Yeah," he said. "I'll calm down."

39

AT 2:45 TULLY WAS OUTSIDE the lodge staring up the slope of the mountain. No sign of the frat boys. He couldn't believe they would be late. He checked his watch again. Five minutes to three. He sighed. Pap came out and stood next to him. The old man took out the makings and started rolling one of his cigarettes.

Tully said, "A couple more minutes and I'll have you roll one of those for me."

The old man snapped his thumbnail on a kitchen match and lit the cigarette. The end of the paper burst into a tiny flame, then died to a glow. Pap blew a cloud of smoke at Tully. "Can't," he said. "These things will kill you."

"Those things are already killing me," Tully said. "I might as well smoke them myself."

"No sign of the boys?"

"Nope."

"Maybe they all got killed in an avalanche."

"Just my luck," Tully said.

He looked at his watch again. One minute to three. He squinted up at the slope. A tiny dot shot out into the open. Then another dot. Finally a third dot.

"Great!" Tully said. "Here they come. And they're on time."

Pap squinted up at the skiers. "I thought there was supposed to be four of them."

"Three is good enough."

The skiers swooped in and slid to a stop in front of Tully and Pap.

"How's our time?" Rodney asked.

"Perfect!" Tully said.

Wiggy and Turk joined Rodney in a cheer.

"How was it?" Pap asked.

"Great!" Turk said. "Exactly like the 3-D map indicated. The guys that made it must have been really good. Maybe I'll switch over to geography."

"Where's Lance?" Tully asked.

"Oh, he's coming," Rodney said. "He took a header into a drift, but he's all right."

Tully squinted up the ridge again, just as another dot zipped into sight.

"Shoot," Tully said. "I thought I'd saved a hundred bucks."

"Keep the money," Wiggy said. "This is the best skiing we've had in years."

Lance slid to a stop in front of them. "These rats left me, and I wasn't even dead," he said.

"Worse yet, Wiggy just told me I could keep the

money I promised you, not that my promises mean anything."

"Hey, the skiing was fantastic!" Lance said. "You saved this vacation for us, Sheriff. I may even apologize to your Indian friend for him beating me up."

"That would be nice. Was my deputy waiting for you?"

"Right where you said he would be. Brian hauled us into town, bought us each a submarine sandwich, and then hauled us up to the Blight Mountain Lodge ski lift. Just as you showed us on the map, it was all downhill from the top of the lift to here."

"You did good," Tully said. "And don't forget, I may need you to testify at a trial."

"Cool!" Turk said. "This gets better all the time."

Tully snapped his fingers in front of Pap. The old man dug in his pocket and pulled out a thick wad of bills. He peeled off four hundreds and gave them to Tully, who dealt them out to the boys. "Now you better lay off the booze the rest of your time here or I'll call your parents. Furthermore, alcoholics make terrible witnesses at murder trials."

"You bet, Sheriff," Lance said.

Tully and Pap went back into the lodge. They stopped at the 3-D map. "My theory proved out like a charm," Tully said.

"I take it you're pretty happy," Pap said.

"Yes, I am. I just proved that a good skier can ski downhill all the way around Mount Blight and do it in six hours. That's plenty of time for Mike to have killed Horace Baker."

"Mike killed Horace Baker?"

"I don't know. I just know that it was possible for him to do it."

"Do we have this case wrapped up?

"We're getting close. Now all we have to prove is who killed Mike."

"I hope that don't take long, because my house-keeper is probably worried about me."

"You mean you haven't called Deedee since we've been up here?"

"Of course not. You never call a woman when you're out on an adventure. Ruins the whole thing."

"You're right. I forgot."

"You didn't call Susan, I suppose," Pap said. "Now that you and her are talking again."

"No, I don't think she regards hearing from me to be all that urgent. I'll probably take a few days off, though, and go on a February camping trip. Think she'd be interested?"

The old man laughed until he was out of breath and in pain. "I see I never taught you to live without hope, Bo," he said at last. "It screws up a man's judgment."

That night Tully ate dinner with Dave. Pap and Lindsay were at another table, the two of them engaged in their usual animated conversation. The old man was dangerous, but better him than Marcus, he thought. Marcus was probably more dangerous to women than Pap. The kid was weak. The worst mistake a woman could make was to marry a weaky, no matter how thin the pickings. Weakies turn women into tigers, and Tully already knew too many tigers.

"You got this crime solved?" Dave asked after the waitress had taken their orders. "I notice you went with the T-bone."

"Getting close," Tully said. "I've got Lindsay working on a list of the guests, to see if any of them stands out for some reason."

"You looking for a hit man up here?"

"It's something I've considered."

"Tomorrow's Sunday," Dave said. "The road is supposed to be open by noon tomorrow. Then everybody is gone, including the hit man or hit men. And best of all, me! As I understand it, the lodge then fills up with dogsled racers."

"Sounds awful," Tully said. "I can't stand the thought of being trapped here with dog people. All they talk is dog. So I've got to get this thing solved by noon tomorrow! You see anybody in this dining room that seems a likely suspect?"

Dave looked around. "How about our three guys over at that table in the corner? Maybe the guy you flattened is the hit man. Arrest him. He seems as good as any, even though he's probably innocent."

"Details, Dave. Details."

40

AFTER HE WAS FINISHED EATING, Tully walked over to Pap and Lindsay's table and took Lindsay by the hand. "I need to talk to you, young lady."

"Can't you talk to me with Pap here?"

"No, I can't."

"He wants to warn you about me, Lindsay," Pap said, smiling.

"Pap is my buddy," she said. "I told you that."

Her crutches were leaning against a chair. Tully leaned them against the wall and sat down across from her. "Yes, you did. But I've known Pap for over forty years, and I can tell you right now he is nobody's buddy."

"That's mean," Pap said.

"Actually, Lindsay, I figure you're smart enough to take care of yourself. What I need to know is if you found anybody on the list that seems to stand out."

"The only ones are those guys in the corner. You flattened one of them the other night."

"I wish people would stop using that word."

"*Flattened*?"

"Yes. Anyway, why do you think one of them might be the hit man?"

"It's not so much the men but the women."

"The women?"

"Yeah, they all look like hookers."

Tully pretended to look casually around the room, taking in the table in the far corner.

"I'm not sure I know what hookers look like," he said.

"*Escorts* might be a better word. You've got to admit the men are a pretty grubby bunch, but the women are all babes. How do a bunch of duds like that end up with three beautiful young women?"

"Happens all the time," Tully said. "But I wonder the same thing."

Lindsay said, "I would have to be paid a whole lot of money even to be seen with one of them."

Tully took another casual look around the room. "I see your point."

"And if you study them closely, you see that the women seem intensely interested in everything the men say. You ever see wives act that way?"

"Can't say I have," Tully said. "I do remember, though, that my wife, Ginger, was always very . . . uh . . . you may be right. Did you get their names?"

"They all registered as if they were married. But that doesn't mean anything. The names could be phony, too."

"Probably are," Pap said. "What we need are fingerprints. Then we can find out who they really are."

Tully called a waitress over. "Do you know who I am?"

"Sheriff Bo Tully," she said, smiling.

"Right. Don't look now, but there's a table over in the far corner of the dining room with six people seated around it, three men and three women."

"The one where you flattened that man the other night?"

Tully sighed. "That's the one. Would you have the busboy not touch that table after the people are gone? And please don't mention this to anyone. Tell the busboy to keep his trap shut, too, or I'll arrest him."

"Yes sir."

"I'm going to collect the drinking glasses from that table, and I don't want the people there to know anything about it. Will you take care of this for me?"

"Yes sir."

"What's your name, sweetheart?"

"Vera."

"Pap, give me a bill."

Pap dug the wad out of his pocket and peeled off a hundred. Tully gave the bill to the waitress. She appeared shocked.

"It's okay," Tully said. "He's rich."

The waitress and Pap beamed at each other. "Thanks!" she said.

"I didn't know you were rich, Pap," Lindsay said after the waitress left.

"Yup," Pap said. "Modestly so."

"I'm the only sheriff of Blight County in a century that hasn't ended up filthy rich," Tully said. "So far I've only accomplished the filthy. It doesn't seem fair."

"Some of us are just more competent than others," Pap said.

"Would you see about collecting the men's glasses from that table," Tully said to Pap. "And keep them in the right order."

"You don't have to tell me everything, Bo."

"You do good work, Lindsay."

"Thanks. Can I stay and help Pap?"

Tully shrugged. "Yeah, I guess a math major can take care of herself."

Walking through the lounge, Tully tapped on the office door. No one answered. He tried the door. It was open. He walked in. Lois had apparently gone to her room. He flopped into her chair and dialed the phone. Herb answered.

"What are you doing there this time of night, Herb?"

"Hey, Bo! To answer your question, running this department is time-consuming. Keeps me working both night and day. I just turned out the night shift. Actually, it's pretty peaceful here right at the moment. Your skiers make it back okay?"

"Yeah, right on time. Brian did a good job. Anyway, I've got some more work for you, Herb."

"How did I ever guess?"

"What we need right now is to tie the gun I found to Mike Wilson. I doubt he registered it with the ATF, but he probably has it listed with his insurance guy.

Would you see if you can track it down with the insurance?"

"You got it, boss. I'll check on that tomorrow. He probably has all his guns listed with the insurance company."

"Let's hope so. What's that noise?"

"Clarence! He barks all day. He's driving me nuts."

"I told you and Daisy to get rid of him!"

"Daisy won't let anybody touch him. She loves that dog. And Clarence loves her. But she split with Albert the Awful, and her new apartment owners won't allow dogs."

"That dog better not be there when I get back. Otherwise he and I are taking a drive deep into the woods."

"Good. That way we'll be rid of Clarence and you'll have Daisy's wrath on you. By the way, the new *Blight Bugle* feature writer stopped by and wrote a feature on Clarence."

"Are you crazy, Herb? Letting him do that? Now we'll have the whole town up in arms if we do Clarence."

"Maybe he could be shot while escaping."

"The feature writer? Let me think about that."

41

TULLY WENT UP TO HIS ROOM. He was exhausted. The two murders were getting to him. He couldn't remember when he had had such a hard time solving a crime. He ran the tub full of hot water. Then he looked through the paperback books stacked on a shelf. The only author he recognized was Danielle Steel. He took the book into the bathroom with him and read it while he soaked in the tub.

It was one of Tully's theories that Danielle Steel probably knew more about romance than all the so-called experts put together. She had sold about a billion books to women all over the world. If she didn't know what women wanted for romance, nobody did. Before he got to the part that might tell him what he wanted to know, he fell asleep and dropped the book in the water.

About midnight he woke up. He had sensed something: the water had turned cold and he was freezing. He got stiffly and painfully out of the tub, put on a lodge bathrobe, and started to shut the window to his room. The wolf howled. It was close this time. He turned out the lights and looked out the window, thinking the wolf might even be in the yard below. Nothing. He looked at the dark wall of trees. Nothing. Then he looked past the tree line into the woods itself. A person stood there. Tully knew who it had to be. The thought passed through his head that he might be looking at a werewolf. If so, the werewolf seemed to be staring directly at his window. Tully stepped back. When he looked again, the figure was gone. He crawled into bed. It was a long time before he went back to sleep.

Snow was still falling the next morning. He heard Grady start up the snowblower and go to work clearing the various paths. There was no traffic in the parking lot, so he knew the road hadn't been opened yet. Supposedly, the county road department had been working night and day to clear the avalanche. He suspected it was probably more like day and day, if he knew the Blight County Road Department. They were not about to pay overtime for the convenience of the sheriff. In any case, he knew that he had until about noon to get the last of the murders solved. All the present guests would pack up and leave, and a new set would arrive. The actual killers might very well be gone within a few hours. At the moment, he didn't have the slightest idea of where even to start. He decided his best bet would be a visit to the logical suspect.

He knocked on the door. Blanche answered. "Hi, Bo," she said. "Come on in. I just made a pot of coffee. You want some?"

"Sounds good." He sat down on her couch.

Blanche went into the kitchen and presently came back with two cups on a tray, cream and sugar, and the pot of coffee. She set the tray on the coffee table in front of Tully and poured the coffee. Tully dumped a dollop of cream in his coffee and added two spoonfuls of sugar.

Blanche sat down opposite him. "You come to arrest me?"

"Not yet, Blanche. I have to admit that I think you're somehow involved, since you are the one who receives four million dollars."

"I know you'll never believe this, but I had no idea those insurance policies even existed. It's awfully hard to prove you don't know something."

"Here's the thing, Blanche, if you're not involved in the murders, there's no point in holding anything back."

"I suppose not."

"I hate to tell you this, but I've had one of my agents watching your apartment. Twice now she has witnessed a man come out of your apartment very early in the morning, like two o'clock."

Blanche bent over and put her head in her hands. She seemed frozen in that position. At last she straightened back up. "I was hoping you wouldn't find out about that. I'm not that kind of woman. Well, I guess I am, but I don't think of myself that way. Mike and I have been essentially separated for well over a year. This thing started several months ago, when Mike pulled one of his disappearing acts. The person is kind and very caring toward me, and I don't want to get him into trouble. He's really a decent person."

"I'm sure, but I need to know who he is."

"Bo, I can't tell you."

"Then I'll have to guess. I'm pretty sure it's DeWayne, your bartender."

"DeWayne!" She broke into a bitter laugh. "He's more like my son, for heaven sakes!"

"I happen to know that he is a Scragg," Tully said. "I've done a lot of business with the Scraggs, none of it good. If somebody commits a crime, I usually start arresting Scraggs until I find the right one. Suppose DeWayne kills Mike and then marries you and the two of you now share the four million. It's perfect. I wish I had come up with the idea myself."

"If you had, Bo, I might have taken you up on it. But I am absolutely not having an affair with DeWayne. He was just a boy when he started working here. He's still a boy! I know all about the Scraggs and most of them are decent, hardworking people."

"I don't know any of those Scraggs," Tully said.

"I suppose not. In any case, I'm not sleeping with

DeWayne. And I certainly would never tell you if I was. You would think I was some sort of pervert."

Tully tugged on the corner of his mustache. "If you don't tell me who it is, I'm going down and grill DeWayne."

"No, please, don't do that. DeWayne knows nothing about this and I don't want him to. Take me to jail first."

"Blanche, I don't want to take you to jail at all, but if you don't give me the name, I'm afraid I'll have to."

"Then you'll have to, Bo, because I'm not giving you the name. Mike's killer could be any of the guests here. Some of them are new people I've never seen before, like the three men at the corner table."

"It could be one of the men at that table, all right, but I'm checking them out as we speak. My agent has informed me that the three women at that table are probably paid escorts. The problem, Blanche, is I doubt there is a connection between those three men and the four million dollars. It's that four million that's causing you all this grief."

"I know it is!"

"And that's why the man who visits your room late at night is of interest to me."

"It can't be him, Bo. He's the kindest, politest, most considerate man I've ever met. But he would never forgive me if I told you who he is."

"Blanche, you just described all the sociopaths I know. Besides, I already have the evidence that should tell me who the killer is."

"Then why don't you arrest him?"

"Because I need to get it back to Blight City and have my CSI unit run some tests on it. If he turns out to be your late-night visitor, I may charge you as an accessory to murder."

"Charge me with whatever you want, but just leave DeWayne alone."

42

SHORTLY BEFORE NOON THE NEXT DAY, a yellow plow truck
came up the road, clearing off the snow. It was followed by a line of cars. The cars pulled into the parking
lot, which was already filled with people packing their
vehicles for the trip home. Tully tossed his plastic bag
of clothes into the backseat of the Explorer and then
walked around and put his duffel in the rear compartment.

He saw Marcus Tripp wave at the driver of a large
Mercedes sedan. The driver didn't look pleased. Marcus got in and he and the driver headed back down the
road. Tully was glad he wasn't riding in that car.

Then Tom Duffy pulled into the parking lot.
He was driving a Lexus SUV. Before arriving at the
parking lot, Tully didn't even know there was such
a thing as a Lexus SUV. He waved and Tom waved

back. Tom parked, got out, and shook Tully's hand. "I hope Janice didn't give you too much trouble," he said.

"No trouble at all," Tully said. "As a matter of fact, I used her and her dog team to help me solve a couple of murders. By the way, I was sorry to hear from Janice that your aunt Margaret died."

Tom looked sheepish. "Yeah, it came on quite sudden. A heart thing."

"A heart thing. Those can be bad. Particularly when you've been dead for, what's it been, twenty years now?"

"You would remember Aunt Margaret!"

"Well, it was such a nice funeral. But you can relax. I never told Janice anything about Aunt Margaret."

"Thank goodness! You always were a good friend, Bo."

Gooder than you'll ever know, Tully thought, smiling.

Janice ran up and kissed her husband. "I hope you're staying for the races."

"Yep, I am. Taking the whole week off. I trust Bo here didn't try to renew old times with you."

"No, unfortunately, he was a perfect gentleman the whole time." She made a quick sour face at Bo behind Tom's back.

"Listen, Bo, maybe you can have dinner with Janice and me tonight."

"I'd love to, but I can't. I've got to drive back to Blight."

Tom nodded. "Yeah, we've been reading all about the murders in the papers."

"In the papers?"

"Yeah, your man Herb Eliot keeps the reading public up-to-date on them. You're lucky to have a person like that in the department."

"Right," Tully said. "Good old Herb."

At that moment Lindsay came up. She let her crutches fall to the ground, kissed Tully on the mouth, and then clung to him, her head resting on his chest. A lean, scholarly-looking man in glasses stepped forward, took his hand, and shook it. "Lindsay is very demonstrative," he said apologetically. "She told me how you saved her life at the risk of your own. I can't thank you enough."

Tully said, "It was nothing I wouldn't do for any beautiful girl."

"You'll call me, won't you, Bo?" Lindsay said into his chest.

"Of course, I'll call you. I have to stay in touch with the best agent I ever had. And I'm almost certain you've helped me solve these murders."

"Really! That is just so cool." She gave him such a powerful hug her dad had to extract her.

"Come on, honey, I've got to get you back to school." Bo picked up the crutches to take back to the lodge. Lindsay's father helped her hop over to another Mercedes.

How come everybody but me is rich? Tully thought.

Blanche came up behind him. "I bet that hot little fox is your agent," she said.

Tully smiled. Blanche was the second woman to refer to Lindsay as a hot little fox. He handed her the crutches. "You could be right about that," he said. "At least the agent part."

"I've been thinking about our conversation earlier," Blanche said. "About my visitor. Sooner or later it will come out anyway."

"You thinking of marrying this individual?"

"That's kind of old-fashioned, isn't it?"

Tully pondered this for a moment. "You going to run off with your lover?"

"What do you think, Bo?"

"I think your secret, late-night visitor, whoever it is, may be my prime suspect."

"In that case, it's good you don't know, and I'm certainly never going to tell you."

"At least think about it," he said. "I should be back tomorrow. If not tomorrow, Tuesday for sure."

She turned and walked up the steps of the lodge. Pap and Dave were coming down; both of them carried bags.

"Where do you two think you're going?"

Dave said, "I've got to get back to my place and start work on my casino. Besides, I've done all I can to solve the murder."

Tully tugged on the corner of his mustache. "So your theory is that a woman put on Mike's rubber boots, made the tracks, then put the boots on Mike. Her accomplice drove a boat up through those horrendous rapids and hauled her back to wherever they docked the boat. Afterward, the killer hauled Mike to the suspension bridge and dropped him in the river."

"That's about it," Dave said.

"I would say that's a bunch of nonsense, except for one thing."

"What's that?"

"It's the only scenario I can come up with. On the other hand, I think a person would have to be a crazy fool to risk running first upstream and then back downstream through those rapids."

"Need I mention that you and Lurch did it?"

"No, you needn't mention that. Lurch's screams are still ringing in my ears."

"So, if you don't need me anymore, Bo, I'm headed to Famine. I enjoyed our little vacation."

"I guess Pap will do for what I have in mind. Hope to see you back for our next murder, Dave."

"You bet!"

"No!" cried Pap. "I've got to get back to my housekeeper. She's worried sick about me."

"Right. She's probably still enjoying her few days of peace. No, you're staying here, Pap. I brung ya and you're dancin' with me."

Dave laughed and walked off toward his SUV.

"You'll like it, Pap," Tully said. "You may even get a chance to kill somebody."

"That's better."

"I'll fill you in when I get back." Tully said.

"And when will that be?"

"Probably Tuesday. We should have this whole business wrapped up by Tuesday night."

Pap went back into the lodge muttering to himself. Then the three women from the corner table came out carrying suitcases. They piled the suitcases in the luggage compartment of a Jeep Grand Cherokee and started to get in. He walked over to them. The blonde who had given him the quick smile at the dinner table had just opened the driver's door.

"You're not leaving the boys behind, are you?" he asked.

"*Boys* is right," she said. "Yeah, they're staying on. Got some unfinished business, I guess."

"How long have you known them?"

The blonde sighed. "A long, long time. About a week."

"I take it you're not too fond of them."

"When you flattened Duke, that was the high point of our week."

"You have any idea why they came up here?"

"Not much. Business of some kind. I don't think it's working out for them."

"I have to take your names," he told her. "Your real names and your real addresses. Just in case I have to get in touch."

"Oh great," she said. She gave him their names and addresses. The addresses were all at the same place near Reno, Nevada. "You want the boys' names? All we have are first names, and they're probably made up anyway."

"Don't worry about it. I'll get their real names. Is it

too forward of me to assume you three are all working girls?"

"You got that right. You ever come down our way, Bo, stop in and see us."

"I'll certainly keep that invitation in mind."

43

WHEN TULLY REACHED THE PLACE where he had rescued
Lindsay from the river, he pulled over to the edge of the
road and got out. The only thing left of the cabin was
its foundation. The BMW was still there, covered with
mud. The access road behind it had been washed out,
so he expected the car would remain there for some
time, sort of a monument to the flood. He was amazed
that the climb up from the cabin hadn't been nearly as
long or as steep as he recalled: something on the order
of a mile or so. It was scarcely a hundred feet. Looking
at the sharp rocks made his knees hurt. Then he started
thinking of Lindsay. He thought of her sitting there
nude in the beam of his flashlight. It made him feel like
a dirty old man, but he couldn't help it. He guessed he
was Pap's son after all. He stopped again to pick up his
light bar and then drove on into Blight City.

Even though it was Sunday, both Herb and Daisy were at the office, along with the usual weekend staff.

"Bo!" Daisy said. For a second he thought she was going to jump up and kiss him. "Herb!" she yelled. "Bo's back!"

Herb came rushing out of his office. "Man, am I glad to see you. This place has been falling apart."

"It's nice to be appreciated," Tully said. "Where's Lurch?"

"Home," Daisy said. "Probably sleeping. He's been working night and day."

"Call him. Wake him up. Tell him to get his butt down here. I need him right now."

"Gosh, already it's starting to feel like old times," Daisy said. She dialed Lurch's number. "Byron, it's me, Daisy. The boss is back. He says for you to get your butt down here right now!"

She listened, then said, "Yeah, well you can tell him that yourself when you get down here." She hung up.

"Daisy," Bo said, "did you get the Playpen shoveled out?"

"Yes, I had the two Scraggs do it. They seemed happy to get out of their cells for a while."

"Speaking of Scraggs, I'd better check on our prisoners. Make sure we haven't lost any of them while I've been gone."

Daisy and Herb gave each other a look.

Tully walked down the stairs to the jail.

"Hey!" Lem Scragg yelled. "We got ourselves a visitor, boys!" The other prisoners came to the bars to look. They shouted out a chorus of insults. A few of them said, "Howdy, Bo," or "How's it going, Bo?" Those were the sycophants and sociopaths. Normal criminals typically expressed their rage at being in jail, much of their ire aimed at the individual who had put them there.

"Hope all you boys have been enjoying yourselves in my absence. You better have your fun now, because I'll be back in a couple days. I understand you haven't been out in the Playpen because the jailer thinks it's too cold. There's no such thing as too cold or too hot for criminals. When I get back you go out if it's eighty below."

This provoked much howling and groaning. Tully laughed.

Stubb Speizer yelled, "Daisy had me kicked out of my own cell. Now I'm sharing a cell with Lister Scragg! It ain't safe! It ain't sanitary!"

"Who did you kill this time, Stubb?" Tully asked.

"I didn't kill nobody. I only cut him a little."

Lister Scragg spoke up. "He stabbed Melvin Tribe three times."

"I caught him kissing my wife!" Stubb said.

"You stabbed a man three times for kissing Sadie?" Tully said. "That's a bit extreme."

"I know, it was stupid, but I was drunk at the time and couldn't think of nothing else to do."

Tully looked up and down the block of cells. "This jail is plumb full," he said. "I've got to get you fellows to trial and off to prison."

"That's harsh, Bo!" Lem Scragg yelled from somewhere.

"It's the Blight way," Tully said.

He stopped in front of a cell. It appeared empty. He looked down. A small brown-and-white dog was peering up at him between the bars.

"Clarence!"

The dog barked.

"Yeah, Clarence!" someone shouted from one of the cells. "Do something about that dog, Bo! He whines and barks all night! We can't get any sleep!"

"Whether you get any sleep isn't high on my list of concerns," Tully said. He stomped out the jail door, up the stairs, and burst into the briefing room. Daisy and Herb looked at him sheepishly. He put his hands on his hips and glared at them.

"I couldn't do it," Daisy said. "Neither could Herb."

"I thought I could, but I couldn't," Herb said. "He's such a cute little fellow."

"He bites people, Herb! He bites little old ladies on the ankles. He hides under their cars and bites them. You're harboring a vicious criminal in that cell. The other ones are bad, but at least they don't bite people, as far as I know."

"You'll just have to do it yourself, Bo!" Daisy said defiantly.

"I have two murders to solve," Tully said. "I don't have time to deal with a dog!"

He walked into his office and slammed the door. A nice fat fly was crawling up the window. He picked up his swatter, whacked it, turned the swatter over, and caught the fly in midfall. Then he dumped the fly into his wastebasket. There had been a time when he would have fed the fly to Wallace, but Deputy Ernie Thorpe had killed the spider, thinking it a threat to Tully's life. Tully missed Wallace a lot more than he let on. One thing about Wallace, no one would accuse him of being cute.

Tully picked up his phone, punched a number, and said, "Herb, get in here."

Herb burst through the door before Tully had even hung up. "Yes, boss?"

"Those calls from the Lodge into Blight, did you do any more work on that?"

"No, boss, I haven't had time."

"Get me the list."

Herb returned a minute later with a handful of papers.

"Here's the thing, Herb," Tully said. "I think someone at the lodge had something to do with the murder of Horace Baker."

"I figured that too, especially after I learned about the key-man insurance. You think it was Blanche Wilson?"

"I don't know. She obviously didn't do it herself. There are three hard cases staying at the lodge, but the avalanche cut everybody off from town. If Blanche was involved, she had to have someone on the outside do it. But after the avalanche it was impossible even to make a phone call from the lodge. Let me see what you got."

Herb handed him the list of phone calls. Tully ran his finger down the page, turned to the next one, checked it, checked the third page. "Not much."

"I didn't think so either."

"You think this might be something?" Tully said. "Somebody from the lodge called the Countryman's Feed Store here in Blight City three times over a couple of weeks."

"Yeah?" Herb said.

"Well, somebody here in Blight had to be involved."

"Somebody at the feed store?"

"What else have we got?"

"Nothing."

"So there you go. And by the way, Herb, I don't want to be reading in the *Blight Bugle* about the murders."

"Geez, boss, the reporters ask questions. What am I supposed to do?"

"How about not answering them?"

44

TULLY DROVE OUT U.S. ROUTE 95 to the Countryman Feed Store. The store was part of a strip mall. The parking lot to the mall was packed with the cars of weekend shoppers. The mall irritated Tully no end, because as a boy he had hunted grouse there when the land was occupied only by thick woods. He refused to shop in any of the mall's stores, even though Dick's Grocery offered the cheapest and best produce in town. He finally found a parking spot and walked over to Countryman's, which was part hardware and part farm supply.

The cashier nearest the door he entered was a cute little brunette. Her name tag said "Bitsy."

"Bitsy," he said, "maybe you can help me out."

"I'd love to, Sheriff," she said, smiling. She had a dusting of freckles over her nose. Tully had a fondness for freckles. He could tell she was already in love with him, even though he couldn't remember having seen her before.

"You must be new here," he said.

"Three years," she said.

"In Blight, that's new. Anybody finds a job in this town, they hang on to it."

She laughed. "That's true."

He checked her hands. No ring on her ring finger.

"I'm not married," she said.

"I'm that obvious, am I?"

She laughed again. "I'm afraid so."

"Now I've forgotten why I came in here," he said. "Oh yes, I was wondering if you sell dog food here."

"Dog food? Nope, we don't. Just farm stuff, like for cattle and hogs and chickens."

"Is the store manager in by any chance?"

"Yes he is. I'll call him for you." She picked up the phone by the cash register. "Mr. Starling, there's a gentleman here to see you at Check Stand five."

Tully stepped back to let a customer pay for his purchases. Presently, a bald man in a blue three-piece suit came hurrying up.

"Yes sir?"

"Hi, I'm Sheriff Bo Tully. I wonder if I could take a few minutes of your time, preferably in your office."

The man's eyes widened in surprise. "Certainly, Sheriff. This way, please. I hope it isn't anything serious."

"Probably not. Just something I have to check out. One of the many nuisances of crime fighting."

Mr. Starling smiled slightly.

They went into a small, tidy office. The manager closed the door behind them. "Yes?"

"I have a criminal investigation under way at the West Branch Lodge," Tully told him. "And as part of that investigation we learned that your store received three calls over a recent two-week period from the lodge. It strikes me as odd that anyone at the lodge would be calling a feed store."

Starling looked puzzled. "I don't recall any calls from the lodge in the past couple of weeks or at any other time for that matter. Three calls, you say?"

"Any of your employees know someone at the lodge, do you think?"

"I have no idea. But wait, I do recall one of our cashiers receiving several personal calls recently. We have a strict policy against that, and I had to speak to her about it."

"Bitsy, by any chance?"

"Why, yes! How did you know?"

"A lucky guess. Look, Mr. Starling, I don't want to get Bitsy into any trouble. I would in fact take it personally if she were to be fired or otherwise caused any problems because of this. Do you get my drift?"

Starling blinked. "Yes, I believe I do. Besides, she promised me it wouldn't happen again. And it hasn't."

"I'm sure it hasn't. Now, I will have to talk to Bitsy about those calls, but I can see that your store is very busy today. So I'll talk to her after work. What time do you close?"

"Six o'clock sharp today."

"Good. I'll speak to her after work."

Tully waited his turn at Check Stand 5 on his way out. He told Bitsy that he would need to talk to her when she got off.

"Good heavens, what about?" she said.

"Nothing too important," he said. "I just need some information I think you might have."

"Weird!" she said.

"Not too weird. I'll see you out front at six. Do you have a car parked out there?"

"Yes, it's that green Toyota sedan." She pointed. "I'll meet you there, if that's okay."

"Perfect."

At five minutes after six, Tully was leaning against the Countryman's Dumpster when Bitsy came scurrying out the back door. "Hi," he said.

Bitsy sagged. "Hi," she said, smiling faintly.

"I ran the plates on the green Toyota," he said. "Not yours. I guess you know what we need to talk about."

"Yes," she said. "I know."

He took a card out of his pocket. "And now I have to read you your rights."

45

LURCH WAS HUNCHED OVER HIS computer by the time he got back to the office.

"Loafing again, were you?" Tully said.

"Sleeping, actually," he said. "Every four or five days I seem to have need of sleep."

"Good, I'm glad you got it out of your system, because I brought you three wineglasses that I want you to lift some prints from. How long do you think that will take?"

"Not long. I suppose you want me to see if I can get matches for them?"

"You must be psychic, Lurch. How long for that?"

"Maybe an hour. Is that quick enough?"

"I guess it will have to be. I'm going to grab some dinner, if I can find someone to eat with me."

"She's still in her office."

"You are a psychic, Lurch."

He called Susan. She seemed happy to hear from him.

"I'm thinking of a tent camping trip in February," he said. "You interested?"

It was cruel, he thought, to make a person laugh that hard, first Pap and now Susan.

"If not a camping trip, then how about dinner at Crabbs tonight?"

"I'd love it!"

Crabbs was the classiest restaurant in Blight City. Each of its tables was covered in a fairly white tablecloth, and each had a candle sticking out of an empty wine bottle.

Tully held Susan's chair for her to be seated, even though the gesture made him feel foolish. Not having to put up with such things was one of the advantages of being married. He hated dating, but what else was there? He was pretty sure that Susan had fallen in love with him. He knew that he had fallen in love with her, but he was careful not to let on. He thought it important not to overplay his hand, particularly after the disastrous camping trip the previous November

"As you can see, I got us our special table," he said.

"I didn't realize we had a special table."

"Yes, indeed."

"We've only had dinner here once before."

"I know. That's why this table is special."

"My recollection is that we sat at the next table."

Tully looked at that table. A young couple was seated there.

"Really? Well, from now on, this will be our special table."

"Is there going to be a from-now-on?"

"That's my plan."

She smiled. "We'll see."

They both ordered prime rib end cuts. The servings were huge.

"I wonder what they did with the other half of the cow," Tully said.

"Please!" she said. "I would just as soon not be reminded that my food once walked around enjoying its life."

"Good point," Tully said. "Do you mind talking a little shop while we eat?"

"Shop is my life. What do you want to know?"

"You still have Mike Wilson's body on ice, of course."

Susan took a bite of her prime rib, chewing it slowly, obviously savoring its juices. "In the cooler," she said. "Of course."

"You said in your report that his nose was broken. I assume that could mean that when he was sapped on the back of the head, he landed on his face."

"That's certainly a possibility, Bo. Even though the skin on his head wasn't broken, he was hit awfully hard. I suspect the killer used something like a bag of lead shot, wrapped in several layers of buckskin. As you indicated earlier, the assailant probably didn't intend for him to die before he was dumped in the river." Susan took another bite of her prime rib.

"That's one of my theories," Tully said. "Now if he

broke his nose when he landed on his face, he probably would have got a nosebleed, right?"

Susan continued chewing but nodded affirmatively.

"Because he was facedown in the river," Tully went on, "all the blood would have been washed away, even from inside his nose."

Susan cut another piece of prime rib. "Right."

"So what I'm wondering is if there would be some way to photograph the inside of his nasal passage to determine if some of the blood vessels were ruptured. That would show that he had bled from the nose. Anyway, could I get a picture like that?"

Susan thought for a moment. "I don't know why not. They get pictures of the inside of the colon with colonoscopy. I think if we got hold of a colonoscope, I might be able to get a close-up photo of ruptured blood vessels in the nose."

The couple at the next table got up and moved.

"I didn't mean to get into colons while we are eating," Tully said.

"That's what happens when you have dinner with a medical examiner."

Tully wondered what it would be like at dinner if he were married to a medical examiner. He might have to give this more thought.

46

TULLY DROVE BACK TO WEST Branch Lodge the following morning. The dogsled races were going full throttle, or whatever full that sled dogs go at. He found Pap at the bar, talking to DeWayne. "He's a Scragg!" Pap said. "Did you know that?"

"Yeah," Tully said. "He tried to tell me not all Scraggs are criminals."

"Well, maybe most of them are," DeWayne said. "A few of us aren't."

"You're the first one I ever met who isn't," Pap said.

"And I'm not too sure about DeWayne," Tully said. "I got a drink here the other night that was a crime."

DeWayne laughed. "That wasn't me that served it, though. I think maybe Wendy picked up a wrong bottle."

Tully said, "DeWayne's boss had this theory that by the second drink a person can't tell good whiskey from bad. So it's a waste of good whiskey to serve single-malt Scotch, say, after the first drink."

"I do what I'm told," DeWayne said.

"Do you know that my great-great-granddaddy hung your great-great-granddaddy way back in the eighteen hundreds?" Pap said.

"No, I didn't."

"And your great-great-granddaddy hadn't even done any crimes yet. But Beauregard Tully figured a Scragg would get around to it sooner or later. So it was kind of a preemptive hanging!"

"That's Pap's favorite joke," Tully said. "Nobody knows if a word of it is true."

DeWayne laughed and poured another shot into Pap's glass. "So how are you coming along on your criminal investigation, Bo?"

"Mighty slow, DeWayne, mighty slow. It's all very complicated. "You're still a suspect, though."

"I figured that much."

"I didn't know DeWayne was a suspect," Pap said.

"Yeah, he is. So I hope you haven't been blabbing any of our investigative findings to him."

"I didn't know we had any investigative findings."

"Actually, we don't."

"Good," De Wayne said. "I probably can get away with it then."

"Probably," Tully said. "By the way, DeWayne, you can help me out a little in that regard."

"I'll do what I can."

"Was Mike Wilson a gun nut? Or did he just have plenty of guns around, like a typical hunter?"

"If by 'gun nut' you mean did he love guns, the answer is yes. He collected some makes and models. I don't know which ones. He was always talking about some gun or other that he had just acquired. I never paid much attention. Sorry I can't be of more help. Even though it may cast more suspicion on me, I'll tell you that I was none too fond of Mike. His murder didn't cause me to lose a bit of sleep."

"That doesn't separate you from the pack," Tully said. "I haven't run into a person yet who cared much for Mike. How do you feel about Mrs. Wilson?"

The glass DeWayne was drying slipped out of his hands and smashed on the floor. He grabbed a broom and dustpan, swept the glass up, and dumped it in a garbage can. "I like her. She's looks after me pretty good."

"How good?" Tully asked.

"You mean are we having an affair of some kind? The answer is no, nothing like that. She's fifteen, twenty years older than I am. She loaned me money, and I'm paying her back, a little at a time."

"Bail money?" Tully said.

DeWayne was silent for a moment. "Yeah, bail money. I did a year for selling weed. But I've been clean ever since. I was a stupid kid. Blanche sent me to bartending classes and gave me a job. She pays me well. Probably about twice what Mike thought I got."

Pap said, "They put people in jail for selling weed? I thought they just required payoffs."

"Some of the feds are picky that way," Tully said. "They even put people away for graft and corruption."

"Now that's carrying law enforcement way too far!" Pap said.

For lunch, Tully reluctantly settled on a tuna salad. Pap took the beef dip with fries. They both took shots of single-malt Scotch. Tully sipped his tentatively. Perfect. He looked over at the bar. DeWayne was smiling at him. He smiled back.

"So what's this job you want me to do?" Pap said.

"Basically, I want you to watch my back."

He laid out his plan.

"Seems a bit risky," Pap said.

"You have a problem with that?"

"Not a bit."

Tom and Janice Duffy came over to their table and sat down. The waitress took their orders, Tom, the crispy chicken sandwich, and Janice, the wild mushroom strudel. They both ordered margaritas.

"Sorry to hear your aunt Margaret died," Tully told Tom.

Tom gave him a quick, hard look. "Yes. She was very old. Always sad, though, when you lose a family member."

"Yes, it is," Tully said. "I remember the last time I saw Aunt Margaret. We were in college then." He estimated Aunt Margaret would now be about 110.

"I never even knew he had an aunt Margaret," Janice said.

"Enough about Aunt Margaret," Tom said. "I understand from Janice that you are in hot pursuit of a murderer."

"There is pursuit but I'm not sure how hot it is. That's one of the reasons I wanted to talk to Janice. I need a favor from her."

"A favor?" Tom said.

"Yes, I need yet another trip up the mountain."

"My pleasure," Janice said, not helping Tully one bit.

"How's the race going, Janice?"

"Fine, I had a great qualifying run this morning, the best time yet. I don't race again until Wednesday."

"Great! "Tully said. "Because tomorrow morning I would very much like you to haul Pap up the mountain. He's a lecherous old devil, but I think you can handle him."

"I like lecherous," she said, giving Tully a look.

Tom laughed. "She surely does."

Tully forced a laugh.

Tom said, "Mind if I ask what's going on?"

Tully glanced around to make sure none of the other diners was within hearing range. He laid out the plan for them.

Pap said, "It used to be a whole lot simpler in the olden days."

"Sure," Tully said. "If you don't mind arresting innocent people."

"I figure everybody is guilty of something."

47

DURING THE AFTERNOON GUESTS CONTINUED to arrive at the lodge, but Tully thought there was a good chance the hot tub would be vacant. He donned his swimming trunks and a bathrobe and went down to the basement. Much to his disappointment the tub was occupied by a gray-haired man and woman. He had turned around and headed back toward the stairs, when the woman called after him. "Oh, sir, there's lots of room in here. Please come join us."

He turned around and came back. "Don't mind if I do. I have a few aches and pains in need of some hot water." He introduced himself, neglecting to mention that he was sheriff of Blight County.

"We're the Fergusons, up from Nevada," the man said, offering his hand. "Ann and Paul."

Tully squatted down and shook the hand. "Hi. I'm Bo Tully." Then he eased himself into the tub.

"Your knees look awful," Ann said. "What on earth did you do to them?"

Tully said he had banged them into sharp rocks while climbing a cliff.

"Good," Paul said. "For a moment there I thought you might be some kind of religious fanatic."

Tully laughed. "Afraid not. So, how long have you folks been married?"

"Twenty-five long years," Paul said.

"Still sleeping together?" Tully asked.

Both of the Fergusons looked shocked. Then Paul said, "Yep, pretty much exclusively, too." He reached over and squeezed Ann's hand.

"Oh, Paul!" Ann said. "You know it's exclusively! I must say, Mr. Tully, you do ask the most personal questions."

"I'm sorry," he said. "I realize it was very impolite, but I had to reassure myself the world hadn't turned entirely upside-down."

"I guess we're getting to be a rarity, all right," Paul said. "You married, Mr. Tully?"

"Nope, my wife died about ten years ago, and I guess I've never found a suitable replacement. It's a lot harder than you might think, Mr. Ferguson. You best take good care of Ann."

"Paul, you listen to what Mr. Tully is telling you," Ann said.

Lois came down the stairs. "Oh, there you are, Sheriff. I've been looking all over for you. Blanche would like you to stop by her apartment when you get the chance."

"Thanks, Lois. Tell her I'll be up shortly."

Lois went back up the stairs.

"Sheriff?" Paul said.

"I'm afraid so," Tully admitted.

"You're Sheriff Bo Tully!" Ann exclaimed. "You're famous!"

"I am?" Tully said.

"In Nevada, anyway," Paul said. "Everybody in Nevada knows of Sheriff Bo Tully."

"Nevada?" Tully said.

"Yes!" Ann said. "Some friends of ours have one of your watercolors. They're very expensive! It's not every sheriff who is also an artist."

"Nevada?" Tully said.

After soaking with the Fergusons, Tully went up to his room and got dressed. His shirt still smelled reasonably good, so he put it back on. He went out to the Explorer and unlocked the .30–30 rifle from its rack. He took a box of shells from the glove compartment and slipped it into his jacket pocket. Then he wrapped the rifle up in a blanket and took it up to Pap's room. He knocked on the door.

"What have we here?" Pap said.

Tully unwrapped the rifle. "You know how to work one of these things?"

"I believe so. Don't you put cartridges or something in it?"

"That's right. And that's the end you point at the target."

"How long has it been since you've sighted in this contraption, Bo?"

"About five years. Why?"

"Just wondering."

"Remember, Pap, you shout a warning first. It doesn't do any good to shout a warning afterward."

"Something like, 'You so much as twitch you're dead'?"

"That's good. And if I get shot first, you don't have to shout anything."

"Goes without saying."

Tully then walked over to Grady's shop. He called out to him several times and, getting no response, wandered around checking out his tools. He opened a door at one end of the shop and found a room full of skis, snowshoes, a toboggan, a couple of sleds, and an assortment of ski boots. He found a yellowish, rubbery roll back in one corner that turned out to be a deflated rubber raft. He had once owned one just like it, a "seven-man" life raft, which apparently meant two men in the raft and five clinging to the outside. It was military surplus. Hanging on a wall nearby were several compound bows, sheaths of arrows, and other archery equipment. Another wall contained numerous kinds and lengths of rope, cords, and even string. A sign on the wall listed various rental prices. One of these days, he thought, I might come up here and rent a pair of cross-country skis. If some frat boys from the city can do so well on them, there was no reason he couldn't.

He walked over to the lounge and poked his head

into the kitchen. Grady and Lois were seated at one of the tables having coffee.

Lois looked up and saw him. "How about a cup of coffee, Sheriff?"

"Sounds good," Tully said. "But don't let me intrude."

"You're not intruding," Lois said. "We're just having our usual afternoon coffee break. But I better get back to the office. Blanche still wants to see you, by the way. She's about to collapse. I'm already running the whole lodge. All the racers are here and now we're getting spectators."

"The races have spectators?" Tully said.

"Oh yes, they're quite popular in fact! You should take some time off and watch them, Sheriff."

"I certainly will keep that in mind, Lois. This could be my new spectator sport, right after NASCAR."

"I bet," she said, going out the door.

Tully sipped his coffee. "I'm afraid I need your help again, Grady."

"You about got Mike's murder figured out?"

"Should nail it tomorrow. I need you to run me up to Cabin Three one more time."

"You seem to be zeroing in on Cabin Three."

"If I'm right, Cabin Three is our murder scene. But that's just between the two of us, Grady."

"Yes sir."

48

BLANCHE ANSWERED HIS KNOCK ON her door. "Come in, Bo. I'm a total mess. After our last visit, I was so upset I was sure you believed I had something to do with Mike's murder."

"What I believe, Blanche, and what I can prove are two different things. It would help a great deal if you told me about your late-night caller."

"I'm sorry, Bo, but I can't tell you. If I thought he had anything to do with killing Mike, I would tell you, no matter how I felt about him."

"Here's the thing," Tully said. "I'm already pretty sure I have the evidence that will point directly to Mike's killer or killers. I do know there had to be two people involved, maybe more. As you are aware, Blanche, at this point you are the only person to profit from Mike's

246

death. You admit that you no longer had any regard for him, and, in fact, that you have a lover."

"Did I say lover?"

"No, but I don't imagine you are visited in the middle of the night by a milkman delivering milk."

"It isn't the milkman," she said. "Anyway, the reason I asked you to stop by is I have to know if you intend to arrest me."

"Do you plan to flee, if I am?"

"I can't flee. I have a lodge to run. But if you are going to arrest me, I need to know. I have to make certain arrangements."

"Do the arrangements have anything to do with the three thugs at the corner table? I notice that the other guests have headed home, but those three are still here, minus the ladies."

"Those people are leaving tomorrow. I informed them I have sold out all the rooms for the dog races. I will need theirs tomorrow."

Tully tugged thoughtfully on the corner of his mustache. "I have to make one more trip up to Cabin Three tomorrow morning. I know that's where Mike was hit on the head. Whoever killed him left some evidence behind. Once I have that, I'm pretty sure I'll have Mike's killer."

"Good. Then I won't have to worry about being arrested."

"I'm not so sure about that. Also, I'm pretty sure you realize your late-night visitor could very well be the person who murdered Mike. You would be his motive, not to mention the four million. If that turns out to be the case, I'm going to arrest you, Blanche, and charge you as an accessory to your husband's murder."

Tully went downstairs to the bar. DeWayne was rearranging some liquor bottles. The man he had flattened was seated at the far end of the bar nursing a drink. He was alone. Tully nodded at him. The man nodded back.

"I see your ladies went home," Tully said to him.

"Yeah," the man said. "Claimed they were getting bored."

"Hard to imagine," Tully said. "Seemed like a pretty fun group to me."

The man gulped the last of his drink and left.

"Not much of a conversationalist," DeWayne said.

"Didn't seem to be."

"I understand you flattened him the other night."

"Yeah," Tully said, shrugging. "I've noticed people aren't too friendly after you do that to them."

"Seems like kind of a rough crowd, those three," DeWayne said. "I'd tend to watch myself around them. I wouldn't be surprised if you're the reason they're staying over for an extra day."

"Maybe they're big fans of sled-dog racing?"

"You really think so, Sheriff?"

"No."

Tully ordered a Diet Pepsi. DeWayne filled a glass with ice cubes and set it and a can of Diet Pepsi on the bar. Tully stared at the can. DeWayne reached over and popped the tab.

"Thanks," Tully said. "I'm getting really tired."

"How's the investigation going?"

"Should about have it wrapped up tomorrow. I know where Mike was killed and how he was killed. I need to pick up some bits of evidence at Cabin Three tomorrow and then I'll know who killed him."

"So I'm off the list of suspects."

"Afraid not, DeWayne. One way or another, you'll know tomorrow."

"Should I pack a bag?"

"Wouldn't hurt."

49

TULLY GOT UP AT SIX-THIRTY the next morning. He put on long underwear, bulletproof vest, wool shirt, black wool hunting pants, wool socks, insulated boots, and shoulder holster. He racked the slide on the Colt Commander .45 to lock and load it. He slipped the pistol into its holster and put on his gray insulated jacket. As a final touch, he put on his black watch cap at a rakish angle. If he wound up dead, he wanted to look good.

Grady was warming up the Sno-Cat by the time Tully got over to the shop. He climbed in next to the handyman.

"Hope this isn't disrupting your schedule too much, Grady," he said.

"No sir, not at all. I've been up since five. Never been much of a breakfast person but I do like my coffee. Have a couple of cups while I watch the news."

Grady started maneuvering the Sno-Cat away from the shop and on up the slope.

"Breakfast just happens to be my favorite meal," Tully said. "So I hope we can get this business wrapped up and be back here while they're still serving."

"Yes sir. Exactly what is this business, Sheriff? Anything I should be worried about?"

"Mostly, I need to pick up some evidence. It's possible, Grady, that there might be some shooting. If you see that kind of situation developing, get out of there fast as you can."

"Yes sir, I plan on doing just that. You think Mike's killer might be up there?"

"It's possible. If he is, there will be shooting. He'll know what I'm after and won't want me to get it."

"If you don't mind telling me," Grady said, "what is the evidence?"

"Can't tell you right now. Maybe on the way back. I actually saw it the other day, but didn't know what I was looking at. You ever do that, Grady? See something but not know what it is you're seeing?"

"No sir, can't say that I have."

When they reached the top of the ridge, Grady turned the Sno-Cat to the left and headed in the direction of the trail and cabin. Tully stopped him a hundred or so feet from the trailhead. He could see the cabin off down the trail. There was no sign of Pap. Grady shut off the Sno-Cat motor. Tully peered into the woods on both sides of the trail.

"Anyone ever teach you to look beyond the tree line when you're out hunting, Grady?"

"No sir, can't say they have."

"That's too bad. Vision naturally stops at the edge of a tree line. Game very often is standing back in the trees. With a little practice, you can teach yourself to see beyond the tree line."

"Yes sir," Grady said. "But I don't hunt."

"Ah, that explains it. Well, at least keep your eyes open, and if you see anything that doesn't look right to you, get out of here."

"Yes sir."

Tully eased himself out of the Sno-Cat and started off down the trail. He would have felt less uneasy if he could have seen Pap peering out from behind a tree. He detected a movement off to his left. He unzipped his jacket. The raven took off. Probably to report to Hoot. Then he heard it. The unmistakable sound of a slide being racked on a semiautomatic pistol.

Shoot, Pap, shoot! Tully's hand reached inside his jacket. He started to spin, to drop to one knee. *Shoot, Pap, shoot! Ginger was coming through the door of their log house. She was smiling, her face bright with perspiration. She held a small bouquet of wildflowers, blue lupine, red Indian paintbrushes, yellow tiger lilies. Shoot, Pap, shoot!* His hand touched the butt of the Colt .45. The Velcro strap snapped loose. *His mother, Rose, blissful with the taste of pie on her lips, smiled at him.* His right knee hit the soft snow. *Ice crystals rose up bright as diamonds.* The Colt was in his hand. *Shoot, Pap, shoot!* The Colt was sweeping up. Grady stood there, his gun leveled at him, his finger on the trigger, his eyes wide either with fear or anticipation. He jerked to one side and fell facedown. Tully could hear the residue of a shot echoing in his ears. A red stain began to spread out into snow from Grady's right shoulder. Pap!

A minute later Pap rushed up, breathing hard. "That was close! So close!" He seemed about to sob.

Tully had sunk back down on his haunches, the Colt loose in his hand. He looked up at Pap. For the first time ever, his father seemed old. His cap had come off and his white hair stood on end. One hand held the rifle, the other trembled, as if struck by some sudden disease of the nerves.

"I'm sorry, Bo," he blurted out. "I was sitting on the bench in the privy when I heard the Sno-Cat. I got up and jacked a shell into the rifle and started to open the door. But the latch had slipped down and the door was stuck tight! I thought about kicking it down but that would make too much noise. I tried to get an angle on Grady through the moon hole in the door but it was too small. So I got out my knife and poked the blade through the crack and shoved the latch up. I swear, Bo, this was the first time in my life I ever got caught unprepared to shoot."

Tully pushed himself up. He walked over to Grady, stuck the toe of his boot under his belly, and turned him over. He reached down and picked up the semiautomatic. He pulled the clip and racked the slide to empty the gun's chamber. The handyman moaned.

"It's okay, Pap," Tully said. "You took ten years off my life, but you got the job done."

Pap stared at him. "I didn't shoot, Bo. I thought you did!"

50

PAP AND TULLY GOT GRADY back to the lodge just as the ambulance was pulling in. Brian Pugh drove in right behind it in a department car. Ernie Thorpe was sitting next to him. The two deputies walked over to Pap and Tully as Grady was being loaded into the ambulance.

"We thought you might be the one you ordered the ambulance for," Pugh said.

"I myself thought that might be the case and wanted to be prepared," Tully said. "Let this be a lesson to you, Pugh."

"Right, Bo. Always be prepared."

"That the fellow killed Mike Wilson?" Thorpe said.

"That's him," Tully said. "I think we can charge him with two murders."

"Two?"

"Yeah, Mike Wilson and Horace Baker. Primary in the Wilson killing, accessory in Baker's."

"How is that possible?"

"I'm not going to tell you, Ernie, because then you'd tell Herb and I don't want to read about it in the *Blight Bugle*."

"That's mean, boss," Thorpe said. "So which one of you shot Grady?"

"Pap," Tully said.

Pap sat down on the front steps of the lodge. He dug around in his pockets and found the makings. Rolling himself a cigarette with shaking hands, he said, "It was a tough shot, too. I had to make it out of the little moon hole in a privy door. Otherwise, I would have hit him in the forehead like I intended and saved the county the expense of a trial. Back when I was sheriff, I always tried to economize like that."

"Even if he didn't save the county money, Pap saved my life," Tully said. "That's worth something."

Pap lit his cigarette, inhaled thoughtfully, and blew a cloud of smoke at Thorpe. "I'll tell you one thing, Ernie, a man has got to think fast and keep a cool head in a situation like that. The first thing I did . . ."

"You can fill in the details later, Pap," Tully told him, reaching down and pulling the old man to his feet. Then he whispered in his ear: "After you've thought them up."

"Good idea," Pap whispered back.

"How about breakfast, old man."

"Sounds good to me. It ain't even eight o'clock yet and already I've done a full day's work."

"Yes, you have," Tully said. He turned to his deputies. "Ernie, you ride in the ambulance with Grady and stay at the hospital with him until I get back. Read him his rights when he regains consciousness. Brian, you wait here. I want you to take care of that little matter for me."

"Right, boss."

As Tully and Pap were going up the steps to the lodge, the three men from the corner table came down carrying their bags. "Guess the vacation is over," Tully said. They glared at him and continued on in silence. They got into a white Chevy Suburban. The driver, the man Tully had flattened, held up one hand as he turned out of the parking lot. Tully waved.

"I don't think he was waving," Pap said.

"Maybe not, but I always like to create good feelings for the sheriff's office. They didn't look much like conscientious voters though."

"Probably not in their entire lives."

Pap went into the dining room to order breakfast for them while Tully stopped by the office to make a phone call. Daisy answered.

"Bo, are you going to make it back today?"

"I hope so, Daisy. You got any deputies in there?"

"Two just walked through the door."

"Good. Did Lurch run the prints on the wineglasses?"

"Yes, he got matches on all of them. All three have outstanding warrants. These are three serious dudes."

"Excellent! Get our guys out to the West Branch

Road and arrest them. They'll be coming down shortly in a white Suburban with Nevada plates."

"We don't have any more room in the jail!"

"Oh, in that case let them go! Daisy, squeeze them in! Or stack them! I don't care how you do it, but get them arrested. Also, send Lurch up here. I've got some more evidence for him to collect."

"You know who did the murders yet?"

"One guy is headed to the hospital right now with a gunshot wound in the shoulder. I'm going to arrest another one pretty quick, the brains behind the outfit."

"You shoot the guy?"

"No, Pap did. Saved my life with a great shot."

"You sound pretty calm. Were you wearing your vest?"

"Sure, but we were close and the guy was going for a head shot. Pap nailed him just in time."

"Can't have a better guy than Pap to back you up."

"Right."

51

LOIS CAME INTO THE OFFICE as he was hanging up. "You're up and working bright and early, Sheriff."

"One of those days, Lois. I haven't even eaten breakfast yet. Right at the moment my mind is occupied with French toast, bacon, and eggs."

"Sounds good to me. I heard about Grady. That is so awful! I haven't told Blanche. I don't think she knows yet. She's been in bed with a terrible headache all morning."

"She's still in her apartment then?"

"Yes, but she's in awful shape."

"I can imagine. But I've got to see her right now."

"You'll have to go up to her apartment then. I'll be gone for a while, Sheriff. Is there anything else you need from me before I go?"

"Not that I can think of, Lois."

Tully found Pap in the dining room, digging into hash browns, scrambled eggs, steak, and toast.

"Hungry?" he said.

"Shooting a man always works up my appetite," Pap said.

Tully pulled out a chair and sat down. "I wouldn't make too much of this if I were you."

"I think I've been quite modest about my heroism," Pap said, spreading orange marmalade on a piece of toast. "And you certainly could show a bit more gratitude, Bo."

A waitress brought Tully's breakfast.

"She's a real cutie," he said, watching her walk away.

"She's got a ring on her finger," Pap said.

"I bet she's married to some lazy oaf lives back in the woods and never works."

"No doubt. Probably one of those oafs who shoot you just for looking at their women. Anyway, Bo, I think you should show a bit more appreciation for me saving your life. It's the only decent thing to do."

Tully leaned across the table. "Actually, your heroism is making me sick to my stomach!"

Pap emitted an evil chuckle and bit into his toast. Talking with his mouth full, he said, "I fired as soon as I had him in the crosshairs."

"The rifle has open sights," Tully said.

"No wonder it was such a hard shot!" Pap said. "By the way, I hope Grady turns out to be the guilty party. I always feel bad about shooting an innocent man."

"Yeah, right! You have such a tender conscience.

His attempt to shoot me is a pretty good indication he's our guy. Anyway, I got Lurch on his way up here to find a bit more evidence."

"I know it's picky, Bo, but you probably should prove Grady was involved with the killings."

The waitress came back with fresh coffee and filled their cups.

"What's your name, sweetheart?" Tully asked.

"Mrs. Phelps," she said, then smiled broadly.

"I'm sorry, Mrs. Phelps," Tully said. "I had hoped the ring was just to keep people like me from hitting on you."

"It doesn't always work," she said, still smiling.

"I guess not," Tully said. "Now, Mrs. Phelps, you're probably wondering why this buffoon across from me is laughing himself silly. It's because he is simpleminded and coarse and always suspicious of my most innocent motives. By the way, and I hope you won't mind my asking this, but is your husband, by any chance, a lazy oaf?"

She looked shocked for a moment, then burst out laughing. "Why, yes, he is! How did you know?"

"A lucky guess."

She went back toward the kitchen, still laughing. Pap shook his head. "You are absolutely the luckiest guy in the world, Bo. Not one in twenty million sick, miserable, desperate bachelors like yourself could get away with a line like that."

"Luck has nothing to do with it. Unfortunately, she walked away before I could ask her if she was divorcing the oaf."

"Enough of your rather pitiful love life," Pap said. "I want you to fill me in on the murders."

"I'll tell you on the way home."

"When's that going to be?"

"In about an hour."

The waitress came back and whispered in his ear. "The divorce is final next month."

He grinned at her. "That's always good to know."

They watched the waitress leave.

"Bo, whatever women see in you, I wish I could bottle it. I'd make a fortune. But to get back to less serious matters, how does Blanche fit into this crime?"

Tully wiped his mustache with a napkin and pushed back his chair. "I'm headed up to see Blanche right now. Go pack the car."

He stopped by the office to see if Blanche had come down. Lois was just leaving. "Blanche is still in her apartment," she said. "She should be down shortly to watch the office."

"You better lock up, Lois. I don't think Blanche is going to feel much like looking after it today."

"You have some bad news for her?"

"I'm afraid so."

"Maybe I should stay then."

"No, it's okay, Lois. I'll look after her."

"All right then. I should be back by noon." She locked the office and went off toward the exit, her high heels clicking briskly. Tully slowly climbed the stairs, pulling himself along with the banister.

He knocked on Blanche's door. She opened it almost instantly. She was wearing a bathrobe and slippers. She ran her fingers back through her hair.

"Oh, I thought it might be Grady."

"I have some bad news for you, Blanche."

"I'm not sure I can stand any more bad news, Bo. But come in and sit down."

Tully went in and sat on the couch. Blanche sat opposite him.

"Well, let's have it," she said.

"Grady's been shot," he said.

"Noooo!"

"He wasn't killed. He's on his way to Blight County Hospital by ambulance even as we speak. It's a shoulder wound."

"Who on earth shot him?"

"My father."

"Your father! Why?"

"Because Grady was about to kill me."

She stared at him, her mouth agape. "He tried to kill you? Why on earth would Grady want to kill you?"

"Because he knew I would be arresting him soon for the murder of your husband."

Blanche was silent for a moment. Then she said, "I'm going to tell you something, Bo. Grady didn't know about it, nobody here knew about it. But I'm selling the lodge. Even before Mike was killed, I planned on getting a divorce and selling out. I have plenty of money, even without the key-man insurance, and I doubt the insurance company is going to come through with it anyway, given two murders were involved. They tend to be suspicious about that sort of thing. I have a nice sunny island picked out in the Caribbean. I'm sick of snow, sick of skiers, and sick, sick, sick of this lodge and its guests—no offense."

"None taken."

"Those three men at the corner table, the ones with the hookers, that's what they were up here for, trying to persuade me to sell it to them."

"They won't be available for a while."

She gave him a questioning look, then nodded. "I see. Well, I had turned down their final offer anyway. They were pretty upset, particularly the one you flattened."

"I suspect they are a lot more upset about now. So do you have another prospect?"

"Yes, I do. A lovely couple by the name of Ferguson."

"Why, I know the Fergusons! I met them in the hot tub, Paul and Ann. They really are very nice. They renewed my faith in the human species."

"And they are quite wealthy, too."

"What do they do?"

"They own a chain of upscale brothels in Nevada."

Tully did not respond.

"So are you going to arrest me now, Bo?"

"Here's the thing, Blanche. I know that neither Mike nor Grady was smart enough to figure out this thing. So there had to be a mastermind behind it."

"And you think I'm the mastermind?"

"Let's walk over to the window for a minute," he said. "I want to show you something."

They walked over to the window and looked down onto the parking lot.

Brian Pugh was leaning against the hood of a Blight County Sheriff's Department Explorer. Lois was in the backseat. They couldn't see the handcuffs, but Tully knew she was wearing a pair.

"Lois!"

"Yep."

"She thought up the whole scheme?"

"Yes, she did."

"So, why are you arresting me, Bo?"

"I'm not, Blanche, unless you can think of something I'm missing."

She leaned against the wall and shut her eyes. "I was so worried!"

"To tell the truth," Tully said, "I was worried, too. I never wanted to arrest you, but for a while there it certainly seemed like I might have to."

"It's a huge relief, but I feel sorry for Lois."

"You don't have to. She and Grady have been a grifter team for a long while, long before they came to the lodge. She was always the brains behind the team. I don't know exactly what their plan was here, but it was not for your benefit, Blanche. I suspect the idea was that you would put the insurance money into the lodge, and she would embezzle it, since she was the one who did the books. Then she and Grady would beat it. Or maybe Grady would somehow talk you into marrying him, and you would shortly thereafter have a fatal accident. Maybe even drown in the river. Now that Mike is gone, you would need more help with the lodge, and who better than Grady? Both Grady and Lois did time ten years ago for ripping off a retirement home and some of the occupants. Lois was the book-keeper. You might want to bring in an auditor to check your books."

"I suppose. One good thing, Bo, now I don't need to tell you anything about my late-night visitor."

"I only need that information now to satisfy my curiosity. Why not tell me?"

"I can't!"

"Is he quite a bit younger than you?"

"Sheriff, it's really none of your business."

52

TULLY CAUGHT DEPUTY BRIAN PUGH in the middle of a yawn as he leaned sleepily against his Explorer. "Not getting enough sleep these days, Pugh?" he said.

"Actually, no. I sure hope I nabbed the right one, boss."

Tully looked in the rear window. Lois glared back at him. "Looks to me like you did. Roll down the window so I can talk to her."

The deputy got in, turned on the ignition, and rolled down Lois's window.

"Hope you're comfortable, Lois," Tully said.

"I don't know why you're arresting me. I know nothing about any of this."

"You mean like plotting out two murders, and maybe even a third one off in the near future. That's not even counting your efforts to kill me and Pap and then kill me again."

Lois shrugged.

"As you no doubt guessed, Lois, I've had you and Grady pretty thoroughly checked out. You have a sheet going back almost twenty years. I don't think our prosecuting attorneys will have too much trouble tying you into this. Grady and Mike had the combined IQ of celery. You were the only one smart enough to think this thing through."

"You trying to flatter me, Bo?"

"You are also the one who wore Mike's boots to make the tracks in the snow."

"Oh, that's a good one."

"Yes, it is. And pretty cold-blooded, too."

She was thoughtful for a moment. "You think I killed Mike?"

"No. But it might be in your best interest to recall exactly how and why both Mike and Horace Baker were killed."

Lois chewed her lower lip. "My lawyer and I will have to think about that."

"Yes, you will," he said. "Lois, I'm afraid I have much more experience with murder than you do. If at some distant time in the future you decide to continue this line of work, take my advice. This whole thing was far too complicated. You were bound to slip up somewhere. Next time you get involved in a murder, simply have your accomplices shoot the party, deep-six the gun, and split."

"I'll keep that in mind," she said, glaring at him.

Tully went back into the lodge. On his way through the lounge, he stopped and took a last look at the three-dimensional map. He thought maybe he should send the EWU geography department a note thanking them for the model. He then walked over to the bar. DeWayne was wiping it down.

"Get you something to drink, Sheriff?"

"A cup of coffee, if you have some made."

"You're in luck," DeWayne said. He poured Tully a cup. Pap walked up and climbed onto a stool. DeWayne set a cup in front of him and poured another coffee.

Tully said, "You got your suntan oil all packed, DeWayne?"

The bartender almost dropped the coffeepot. "Why would I need suntan oil?"

"Oh, I just figured that after the dogsled races you'd head for someplace warm and sunny, like the Caribbean, for example."

DeWayne slowly and carefully set the coffeepot back on its warmer. "Sounds like fun," he said. "But you must be confusing me with someone else."

"I suppose," Tully said. "It was just a thought."

Pap dumped two spoonfuls of sugar into his coffee. "Forget the Caribbean. Right now I'll just be happy to get back to Blight. Never thought I'd ever say that."

"Pap and I are gonna head in shortly, DeWayne. From now on, you'll have to flatten any unruly customers yourself."

"One of my major joys in life."

Tully noticed Janice sitting at a table in the dining room. A waitress brought her a pot of tea and left. Tully walked over and sat down across from her. "So, how come you're not out on the trail?"

"My next run isn't scheduled until this afternoon." She gave him a smile. "Tom went home, by the way."

Tully thought about asking if Aunt Margaret had died again but decided against it. "I guess he doesn't have much interest in your passion," he said.

"My passion?" she said.

"Dogsled racing."

She laughed. "No, he doesn't."

"Anyway, I wanted to thank you, Janice, for all your help. You've been great."

"I can be even greater, Bo."

"You've mentioned that. But Pap is waiting for me."

"Have you noticed how stuffy it is in here?"

"As a matter of fact, I have."

"Why don't we step out onto the veranda for a breath of fresh air?"

"Okay," he said. "One last breath."

They went out onto the veranda. Tully closed the door behind them.

Janice kissed him so long and hard he felt as if she had sucked away half of his oxygen. He gently shoved her back.

"I love you, Bo," she said.

"I have a problem with that."

"What?"

"I love you, too. So we can't ever do this again."

53

DRIVING BACK TO BLIGHT CITY, Tully felt as if Janice's kiss would affect him for the next six months. Well, at least for an hour. At every possible place to turn around, he slowed down.

"What's wrong with you, anyway?" Pap said.

"Loss of oxygen," Tully said.

Pap rolled himself a cigarette and punched in the dashboard lighter. "Now, tell me how you've got this caper all worked out."

"I was hoping you might ask. First of all, the avalanche was deliberately set, for two purposes. One was supposedly to isolate from town everyone on this side of the avalanche. It was avalanche as alibi for murder. That way anyone on the lodge side of the avalanche wouldn't be suspected of murder, even if they had a motive."

The lighter popped out. Pap lit his crooked little cigarette. "Well, it fooled me."

"It would have fooled me, too, except that when I first met him, Grady volunteered the information that Mike Wilson had apparently driven the Sno-Cat while Grady was in town. He was covering his tracks, or more specifically, the Sno-Cat's tracks. Later I would discover that those tracks ran all the way to the end of the ridge above the lodge. I couldn't think of any reason why anyone would run the grooming machine way out there, when no one skied out there."

"So why did Wilson run it out there?"

"Would you mind rolling down your window, so your lethal-smelling smoke goes out your side, instead of into my lungs?

The old man cracked his window. "Satisfied?"

"Not really. Anyway, while I was looking at the 3-D map one time it occurred to me that someone like Mike could ski downhill all the way to Blight and then ski downhill all the way back. But Grady had to drive him out to the end of the ridge in the Sno-Cat. Otherwise it would take Mike too long to get into Blight and back. Then Grady had to bring the vehicle back to the lodge. Grady was covering up his part of the scheme, in case I started wondering about the track out to the end of the ridge."

They came to the spot where Tully had rescued Lindsay and Marcus from the cabin. "Hard to believe the river was such a menace that night," Pap said. "Anyhow, I've figured out how he got back. He rode the Blight Mountain ski lift to the top of the mountain.

Then he was able to ski downhill all the way back to the West Branch side."

"That's right. The one weakness in the plan was they had to bring another person into it, to pick Mike up at the base of the mountain, haul him to Baker's office, and then up to the ski lift before it shut down at one a.m. That was Bitsy."

"Bitsy?"

"There were three calls from the West Branch Lodge to Countryman's Feed Store. Why would anyone from a lodge be calling a feed store? It was because of Bitsy. Wilson made the three calls to make arrangements with Bitsy."

"Shucks, I know Bitsy!" Pap said. "I must have bought five hundred pounds of chicken feed from her."

"You don't have any chickens."

"What has that to do with anything?"

Tully shook his head. "It never stops, does it?

"Nope."

"Anyway, I don't think Bitsy had any idea Wilson intended to kill Baker, but she had to know afterward. She's the one who can tie Wilson to the Baker murder."

"And we have the gun that killed Baker," Pap said.

"Yeah, and just as I thought, the gun turned out to be registered with Mike's insurance company. He may have been a tough guy, but he had a soft spot for guns. He couldn't bring himself to dump an original Colt Woodsman."

"How did Bitsy get involved with these bad guys anyway?"

They came to the site of the avalanche. Tully pulled

over and stopped. "I think Grady set her up. My theory is that he had been dating her for a month or two."

"Bitsy wouldn't date somebody like Grady!"

"You may not know it, Pap, but the pickings are pretty thin these days in the man department. She can tie Grady to the scheme and Mike, too. So I suspect Bitsy wasn't long for this world either."

Both of them got out and looked at the remains of the avalanche. Snow, rock, and trees had been cleared from the road and dumped over the edge at a place where the river curved out away from the mountain.

Tully said, "It was all the rock and trees in the avalanche that made me think this thing had been manufactured. I don't know much about avalanches but my impression is they consist almost entirely of snow. Mike, Grady, and Lois had been planning this thing for quite a while. Mike had found some holes in a rockslide up by the ridge and covered them up before the snow fell. Then he went back, uncovered them, and placed the ditching dynamite down in the rocks. When the dynamite went off, it ripped everything loose, snow, ice, rock, trees, everything. When it became clear the avalanche had been started by someone, I figured the main purpose was to kill us. My impression was that Blanche was the only person who knew when we would be coming along the road. Then I remembered that Lois had been sitting right next to her."

"So Grady stopped the Sno-Cat up on the ridge, and he and Mike waited for us to come along. Mike set off the dynamite, and then Grady drove him out to the end of the ridge."

"Yep. He could have used the night-vision glasses to make sure it was us."

They got back in the Explorer. "So why did Grady kill Mike Wilson?" Pap asked.

"Greed," Tully said. "Two million wasn't enough for them. They decided to go for four. The three of them had conspired to kill Horace Baker for the key-man insurance. Then Mike probably mentioned he had key-man insurance, too. Lois decided four million dollars was better than two million. They would figure out later how to separate it from Blanche."

"You don't think Blanche was in on it then?" Pap said.

"No, even though she certainly had the motive. In any case, she would have been another victim before this thing was over. Lois probably had already separated her from a considerable sum. But even without the insurance money, I think Blanche has far more than she'll ever need or want. That goes for DeWayne, too."

"What! You think DeWayne is her lover?"

"Not her lover. Her son. He was born out of wedlock when she was a teenager. The father's family took him and raised him."

"Scraggs?"

"Yeah, some of the good Scraggs."

"You think DeWayne knows?"

"Maybe not," Tully said. "But I bet Blanche is taking him to the Caribbean with her. Probably intends to set him up with his own little beachfront bar. Sounds pretty good. I wish she was taking me."

"Me, too!" Pap said. "So Lois put on Mike's boots and made the tracks from the lodge to the river. And Grady picked her up in the jet boat."

"I'm not so sure about that now."

Pap stared at him. "You don't think Grady picked up Lois in the boat?"

"Grady is stupid, all right, but I don't think he's that stupid. A person could get himself killed driving a boat up through those rapids."

"That was my opinion. But the person making the tracks couldn't get to the river and then float up into the air. Hey, here comes a sheriff's vehicle."

"It's my CSI unit."

Lurch pulled up alongside them and rolled down his window. "You got the murders all wrapped up, boss?"

"Pretty much, Lurch. Tomorrow the department will be back to normal."

"I was afraid of that. So what is it you want me to check?"

"There's a toboggan in the rental room of Grady's shop. I think I detected some tiny spots of blood on it that should match Mike Wilson's. I'm pretty sure Grady used that toboggan to haul Mike's body to the river. He couldn't have carried it."

"Anything else?"

"Yeah, Cabin Three up on the mountain is where Wilson was hit over the head. There's a stain where I think his nose hit the floor. See if you can get a big enough sample to have his DNA in it."

"By the way, boss, the state crime lab picked up both Wilson's and Grady's DNA on the same piece of evidence the cleaning lady took out of the cabin. That should nail Grady for the murder."

"Great! See you later, Lurch."

The CSI unit drove on up the road.

"What evidence is that?" Pap said.

"Sunflower-seed shells."

"Sunflower-seed shells?"

"While Grady was waiting at the cabin for Mike to return from murdering Baker, he calmed his nerves by chewing sunflower seeds and blowing out the shells. When Mike fell and broke his nose, he splattered some blood on the shells. So we've got both his and Mike's DNA on the same shells."

Pap shook his head. "Technology is taking all the fun out of crime."

"It has done that," Tully said. "So what do you think of my crime solving, Pap?"

"Fair to middling. That's how I had it figured all along. You can't do better than that."

54

TULLY DROPPED PAP OFF AT his house. Deedee ran out and gave the old man a big kiss. His cap actually flew off and landed in the snow. Deedee picked it up and slapped it back down on his head. Then she took him by the arm and led him up on the porch. Before going in the door, the old man turned and gave his son a grin. Tully thought maybe he could use a housekeeper himself.

The next morning, as usual, he found Herb sitting on the edge of Daisy's desk. "That's exactly where I left you, Herb," he said. "How does Daisy get any work done with you around?"

"Bo! You're back!" Daisy cried.

"I hate to admit it, boss," Herb said, "but even I'm glad to see you." He walked over and shook Tully's hand.

Tully looked over in the corner of the briefing room. "Where's Lurch?"

Daisy said, "He's probably home sleeping."

"I don't allow Lurch to sleep. Call him up, Daisy, and get him down here. Where's Pugh?"

"He went out to get breakfast."

"I don't allow Pugh to eat. Get him back here."

He walked down to the women's jail and asked the matron, Lulu Tate, if Lois was decent.

"About as decent as she gets," Lulu said. "That broad has a really bad mouth on her. We got her into a nice orange jumpsuit and fixed her a nice breakfast this morning. Apparently she didn't find the chunk she took out of Brian's arm yesterday all that filling."

"She bit him?"

"Yeah, but I disinfected him and bandaged him up. He's pretty cute for a deputy, but he squeals like a pig when you pour disinfectant into a bite. You need to toughen up your deputies, Bo."

"I'm working on it, Lulu. Bring Lois out here, will you? Put some cuffs on her first."

"I should put a muzzle on her." Lulu walked back to the cells and shortly returned with Lois, her hands cuffed behind her.

"They treating you all right, Lois?" Tully asked.

"What do you think?"

"Oh, yeah, that's right, they put you in jail. Other than that, Mrs. Lincoln?"

"I'm glad you think this is so funny."

"Actually, I don't. Jail is about the most boring

thing I can think of. Prison is almost a relief, when you get moved up to it. But you already know that."

"It sounds kind of familiar," she said.

"Here's the deal, Lois. I've got you nailed six different ways from Sunday. If you help me confirm a few details, though, I'll do what I can for you with the judge. You'll probably still do twenty years, but maybe I can get you in a nicer prison and a job where you can help with the bookkeeping or something."

Lois rolled her eyes. "What is it you want to know, Bo?"

"For one thing, what happened at Cabin Three. The way I've got it figured, you, Grady, and Mike arranged to meet at the cabin after the murder of Baker. Mike skied in about three that morning. He went into the cabin, filled you in on what happened, and at some point Grady hit him in the back of the head with a sap."

"That's about it. He wasn't supposed to hit him so hard that it killed him, though. Grady is seriously stupid."

"I know. You wanted Mike to live long enough to drown in the river. You had a pair of Mike's rubber boots in the shop. You put them on and made the tracks from the Pout House to the river. You later removed Mike's ski boots, and put the rubber boots on him. Then you loaded Mike on the toboggan in the rental room, and Grady hauled him up to the middle of the suspension bridge on the toboggan and threw him off. That's why the flat track of the toboggan is lighter coming back over the bridge than it is going out."

"What do you need me for, if you think you know it all?"

"I just need it confirmed."

"You got it about right. But I didn't know Grady and Mike were going to do any killing."

"Sure. Okay, Lulu, you can take her back."

"You promised to help me, Bo," Lois yelled back at him as she was being led away.

"I never go back on my word, Lois. Also, keep in mind that neither deceased was greatly loved. You may even get an award for helping dispose of them."

He pulled out Lulu's chair and sat down in it. When the matron returned, he asked her to bring out Bitsy.

"You want her cuffed, Bo?"

"No, she's harmless."

Bitsy wasn't nearly as cute as he remembered. Her orange jumpsuit was too big for her and her hair was a mess. He jumped up and offered her the chair. She sank into it.

"They treating you okay, Bitsy?"

"I guess," she said. "I've never been in jail before."

"Yes, you have," Tully said. "Once you did a couple years for passing phony twenties."

"Oh that?" she said.

"Yep. Anyway, if there is any possibility of your going straight, I may be able to get you out of this mess. I suspect you didn't realize that Mike was going to shoot Horace Baker when you drove him over there."

"I didn't!"

"But you knew something was up."

"Yeah."

"Did Grady set you up for this?"

She nodded her head yes. "I was supposed to get a thousand dollars for picking Mike up, taking him to Baker's, and then hauling him up to the Blight Mountain Lodge so he could hop on the ski lift. I work almost a month at Countryman's for that much. But I've been going pretty straight since the counterfeit mess."

"I'm glad to hear it, because I'm going to let you go, Bitsy, even though I'm aware that the next day you had to realize that Mike had killed Baker. Countryman's will keep you on, I'll make sure of that. So don't try to run."

"Gee thanks, Sheriff! I didn't expect this."

"I would do the same for any pretty woman. But you better not skip out on me, Bitsy. I need you to get up on the witness stand and tell the truth. If I have to hunt you down, you'll be very, very sorry."

"I'll be good."

"I hope so."

After signing for Bitsy's release, Tully walked over to the men's jail. As usual, he created a considerable row among the inmates.

"Just making sure you're all being treated humanely!" he yelled above the noise. That only increased the volume. Several of the inmates were dragging tin cups along the bars, something they had seen in prison movies. Stubb Speizer yelled, "Bo, you got to get me out of this cell with Lister Scragg. He's killing me!"

"How come you're not back in your own cell, Stubb?"

"Because Daisy is keeping that stupid dog in there!"

"What!" Tully said. "Clarence is supposed to be nonexistent by now."

"Well, he ain't! He's still in my cell!"

Tully walked over and looked down at the little dog. Clarence growled at him.

"See what I mean, Sheriff. I'm thrown in with Lister, and a dog gets a whole cell to himself!"

"Shut up, Stubb!" Then Tully yelled at the jailer. "Hank, find me a length of rope. I guess I have to take care of this myself."

Tully walked into the briefing room dragging Clarence behind him. The little dog skidded along on his hindquarters.

"Stop, Bo!" Daisy cried. "You're hurting him!"

"I'm not hurting him. If he would walk along like a decent animal, there wouldn't be any problem at all."

"What are you going to do with him?"

"Only what I asked you to have done, Daisy. Now I have to do it myself. You knew better than to leave this up to me."

"But he's so cute, Bo!"

"Daisy, we've been through the cute thing before. He bites people. He bites little old ladies. Townspeople hate him. Idiots shoot at him with high-powered rifles right in the middle of town. Worse, they miss! Somebody is going to get killed. Clarence has created a reign of terror around here for the last six months, and I'm putting an end to it."

Daisy's eyes welled up and she dug around for a Kleenex.

Lurch came through the door. He had big circles under his eyes and his hair was standing on end. Tully thought he looked better than usual. "What's going on?" Lurch asked, looking around.

"Bo is going to kill Clarence!" wailed Daisy.

"Oh, that," he said.

"You get the evidence I asked for, Lurch?"

"Yeah, boss. The drops on the toboggan in the rental room were blood, all right. I'll get their DNA checked. The stain in Cabin Three was also blood. Might be able to get the DNA on that, too."

"Good. By the way, Lurch, here's something you'll find amusing. I don't think Grady used the inflatable boat to pick up Lois."

"No!"

"Yes! I got to thinking about our trip up the river and decided that Grady would have thought it far too dangerous."

"Don't tell me any more, boss!"

"Perhaps you remember, Lurch, that the river was quite mild where the tracks were!"

"No! Stop!"

"I think what happened was, Grady towed her across the river in a rubber raft."

"How would she get a rubber raft? She couldn't carry it out with her."

"Grady had it on the other side. You remember when Pap found that arrow near the river? Well, Grady shot it across from the other side. It had a string tied to it. Then Lois pulled a rope across the river with the string. Then she pulled the raft over with a rope."

"Stop! I can't stand this!"

"Finally, she got in the raft and Grady pulled her back across the river with another rope attached to the raft!"

"So we risked our lives for nothing!"

"We found Mike's body, didn't we? That's something. But at least we know now Grady isn't totally stupid. He didn't try to run up the river in a jet boat."

"Yeah, we know that!"

"I do hate to send you back up to the West Branch Lodge, Lurch, but I think you may find Lois's fingerprints on the raft. It's rolled up in the lodge's equipment rental room."

"Anything else?"

"Yes. Get some sleep one of these days, Lurch. You look terrible."

"I'm surprised you don't want me to do Clarence in my spare time."

"I can do Clarence myself. He and I are taking a ride out into the woods right now."

"Men!" Daisy said. "I'm the only one who cares about you, Clarence!"

Clarence, sitting on his hindquarters, glanced casually around, probably for some ankles to bite. Tully walked out the briefing-room door. The little dog slid along behind him.

"So long, Clarence!" Herb yelled after him.

"Bo is so cruel!" Daisy said.

Herb sat down on the edge of her desk. "Yeah, he is that all right."

"Shut up, Herb!"

55

THE CLARENCE SITUATION HAD BOTHERED him a lot more than he had expected. He had killed men without losing a wink of sleep. Clarence still gnawed at him. The little dog had sat there, staring up at him with those defiant big brown eyes. Tully hated the whole concept of cute even more now. It kept men from being men and doing what they had to do. To clear his mind, he finally decided to pack up his watercolors, his tent, and his sheepherder stove, and head up the West Branch for a few days of painting. Maybe it was time for him to devote himself full-time to art.

He called Susan and asked her if she wanted to go along, even though it was February. Surprisingly, she seemed receptive. "Let me think about it. I can't believe I'm saying this, but camping out with you in February almost sounds like fun."

Then Janice called from Boise. Another of Tom's relatives had died, this time up in Idaho Falls. She was all alone, she said. He knew Janice was definitely an outdoor type, and he still hadn't recovered from that last kiss. Just talking to her brought back some delicious memories from their college days. While he was pondering Janice, Lindsay called from her dorm at Washington State University. She said she couldn't keep her mind on her math, thinking about him. "Since we've already been intimate once," she said, "I don't think it would hurt if I came down to Blight for the weekend."

"But I'm going camping up the West Branch," he said.

"Perfect!" she said.

Tully wasn't quite sure what to do with this embarrassment of riches. Life could get so complicated. Aside from other matters, the weather along the West Branch turned out to be perfect for painting: no snow or rain, and a nice mist hung over the river for days. The sun occasionally broke through and created whole new dimensions in the landscape. In three days, he did almost a dozen watercolors, some of them excellent. He believed every watercolor attempted was a gamble, but the more you painted the better the odds a few would turn out first-rate.

He took the fourth day off and waited up on the road for Jennifer and her bookmobile. He stood in the middle of the road and flagged her down.

"Hi, I'm Bo Tully, sheriff of Blight County," he told her.

She seemed a bit surly. "I know who you are. What do you want?"

"I need a ride," he said. "What do you think?"

He climbed into the seat alongside of her. Rather irritably, or so he thought, she stepped on the clutch and shoved the stick shift into low gear. The ancient transmission bucked up in the floor every time she shifted. Tully wondered vaguely if he could still drive a stick-shift. Obviously, if a woman with streaks of gray in her straight brown hair could handle such a machine, he was pretty sure he still could. To be kind, Jennifer was plain. He wondered about Hoot's fondness for her. Probably all those years alone in the woods, he thought.

"You read books, Sheriff Tully?" Jennifer asked.

"I read one once," he said. "But I got pretty sick of the stupid dog, the one they called Spot."

Jennifer smiled. "I suspect you've read more than that."

"Let me put it this way, I don't have a TV. My evenings are pretty lonely."

"I doubt they're all that lonely, from what I hear through the gossip mills."

"My mother is in charge of the Blight County gossip mills," he said. "No rumor makes the rounds unless Ma approves it. She has single-handedly raised my reputation as a ladies' man to astronomical levels. So, you married, Jennifer, or do you just wear that ring to keep strange men like me from hitting on you?"

"Yes, I got married right out of high school. His name is Jesse. He's a mechanic."

"Why, I know Jesse. He's not even a lazy oaf."

"No, he isn't."

"He's fixed my car a few times. He did an excellent job, but charged me for it, apparently not realizing how things are done in Blight."

She laughed. "I didn't say he was perfect."

"I have to admit that you found yourself a good one, Jennifer. So are you and Jesse happily married?"

"I hope so. We do okay. Our boy is a freshman at the U of I. So what do you want with Hoot?"

"Hoot who?"

"You know Hoot who. There's only one Hoot, and I can tell you right now, he won't be happy to see you."

"Probably not, but that's the reason I'm riding along with you. Otherwise, I wouldn't see Hoot at all."

"I hope you're not thinking of arresting him. If so, you can get out right now."

"I'm not going to arrest him, Jennifer."

A couple of miles past the West Branch Lodge, Jennifer pulled into a turnout and shut off the engine.

"What now?" he said.

"We wait. He may not show up, if he sees you here. And there's no doubt he'll see you. Open your door."

Tully opened his door.

They waited in silence for many long minutes. Suddenly, Hoot was standing next to Tully. He had his rifle cradled in his arms, one finger resting against the trigger guard.

"What are you doing here, Bo?"

"I'm glad you asked that, Hoot. I brought you a present." He handed the mountain man a package.

"A present?" he said, leaning his rifle against the

bookmobile. "I don't need a present. I don't want one, either."

"Open it," Tully said.

Hoot tore off the wrapping and stared at the gift. He smiled. "Two leather-bound volumes of Willy's plays! You shouldn't have, Bo."

"I figured I owed you something, Hoot. It certainly isn't an award for your marksmanship, but I have to admit, you shoot well enough."

Hoot was silent, staring at the two volumes. Then he said, "These old eyes aren't quite what they used to be. But I understand what you're saying.'

"Well, I don't!" Jennifer said.

"The books aren't an expensive gift, Hoot. I got them cheap, at an English professor's estate sale. I understand he was a major Elizabethan scholar and had scribbled little notes all through them. Otherwise, they're in pretty good shape. I didn't think you would mind, having them all marked up like that."

Hoot laughed. "No, I don't mind at all."

Jennifer said to Hoot, "I guess you won't be needing my Shakespeares again, Ben. Can I interest you in something else?"

"Actually, that's why I came down, Jenn, even with Bo here. I'm moving on."

"Moving!" she gasped.

"Yep, the mountains and the winters are getting too hard for these old bones. I've got myself a nice remote island in the Caribbean picked out. Figured I'd spend the rest of my days lying on a warm, sandy beach, reading my Willys, of course." He smiled.

"The Caribbean?" Tully said.

"Don't expect a postcard, Bo."

"I won't. At least not from you."

Hoot stared at him for a moment. Then he winked.

That night Tully cooked a nice dinner for two on the sheepherder stove. Then they turned in early. Bit by bit, all the mental and muscular knots loosened and finally disappeared. His painting couldn't be going better. He was even starting to think of himself as an artist. For the first time in years, he was beginning to relax. He was almost asleep when he felt the soft warm body snuggle up against his back. Then the wet tongue was in his ear. Teeth brushed against his shoulder.

"Nibble, Clarence, nibble!" he shouted. "Don't bite!"

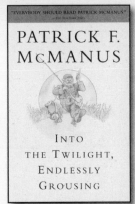
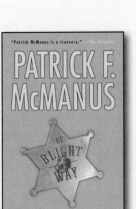